THE W~~HISPERS OF LO~~VE

The Marquis had never noticed how large and lovely her eyes were, but now that they were so close to him he could not avoid their impact.

"Lexia – " he started uncertainly. "I want to – "

"What?" she whispered.

No more words would come. His heart was thundering and the world seemed to be turning about him and suddenly he was unsure of everything that had been so clear earlier.

Gradually he began lowering his head.

She did not reach up to him, but neither did she pull away. She seemed transfixed, her eyes gazing into his as though she was waiting – hoping – for something.

In another moment his lips would touch hers.

And then reality burst in, shattering the pleasant dream that had been slowly enveloping him.

This was a betrayal.

THE BARBARA CARTLAND PINK COLLECTION

Titles in this series

THE WATERS OF LOVE

BARBARA CARTLAND

Barbaracartland.com Ltd

THE BARBARA CARTLAND PINK COLLECTION

Barbara Cartland was the most prolific bestselling author in the history of the world. She was frequently in the Guinness Book of Records for writing more books in a year than any other living author. In fact her most amazing literary feat was when her publishers asked for more Barbara Cartland romances, she doubled her output from 10 books a year to over 20 books a year, when she was 77.

She went on writing continuously at this rate for 20 years and wrote her last book at the age of 97, thus completing 400 books between the ages of 77 and 97.

Her publishers finally could not keep up with this phenomenal output, so at her death she left 160 unpublished manuscripts, something again that no other author has ever achieved.

Now the exciting news is that these 160 original unpublished Barbara Cartland books are already being published and by Barbaracartland.com exclusively on the internet, as the international web is the best possible way of reaching so many Barbara Cartland readers around the world.

The 160 books are published monthly and will be numbered in sequence.

The series is called the Pink Collection as a tribute to Barbara Cartland whose favourite colour was pink and it became very much her trademark over the years.

The Barbara Cartland Pink Collection is published only on the internet. Log on to www.barbaracartland.com to find out how you can purchase the books monthly as they are published, and take out a subscription that will ensure that all subsequent editions are delivered to you by mail order to your home.

NEW

Barbaracartland.com is proud to announce the publication of ten new Audio Books for the first time as CDs. They are favourite Barbara Cartland stories read by well-known actors and actresses and each story extends to 4 or 5 CDs. The Audio Books are as follows :

The Patient Bridegroom	The Passion and the Flower
A Challenge of Hearts	Little White Doves of Love
A Train to Love	The Prince and the Pekinese
The Unbroken Dream	A King in Love
The Cruel Count	A Sign of Love

More Audio Books will be published in the future and the above titles can be purchased by logging on to the website www.barbaracartland.com or please write to the address below.

If you do not have access to a computer, you can write for information about the Barbara Cartland Pink Collection and the Barbara Cartland Audio Books to the following address :

Barbara Cartland.com Ltd.
Camfield Place,
Hatfield,
Hertfordshire AL9 6JE
United Kingdom.
Telephone:+44 (0)1707 642629
Fax:+44 (0)1707 663041

THE LATE DAME BARBARA CARTLAND

Barbara Cartland who sadly died in May 2000 at the age of nearly 99 was the world's most famous romantic novelist who wrote 723 books in her lifetime with worldwide sales of over 1 billion copies and her books were translated into 36 different languages.

As well as romantic novels, she wrote historical biographies, 6 autobiographies, theatrical plays, books of advice on life, love, vitamins and cookery. She also found time to be a political speaker and television and radio personality.

She wrote her first book at the age of 21 and this was called *Jigsaw*. It became an immediate bestseller and sold 100,000 copies in hardback and was translated into 6 different languages. She wrote continuously throughout her life, writing bestsellers for an astonishing 76 years. Her books have always been immensely popular in the United States, where in 1976 her current books were at numbers 1 & 2 in the B. Dalton bestsellers list, a feat never achieved before or since by any author.

Barbara Cartland became a legend in her own lifetime and will be best remembered for her wonderful romantic novels, so loved by her millions of readers throughout the world.

Her books will always be treasured for their moral message, her pure and innocent heroines, her good looking and dashing heroes and above all her belief that the power of love is more important than anything else in everyone's life.

"Love knows no barriers, accepts no obstacles, recognises no reverse and is always resplendent in its own glory."

Barbara Cartland

CHAPTER ONE
1898

It was a high fence but the horse took it easily, landing lightly on the other side and causing the rider to break into a smile.

"Well done, old fellow," he said, patting the animal's great neck.

Man and horse were pleasant to behold, both handsome, both in the prime of their youth and vigour.

Francis, Marquis of Wimborton, took a ride every morning at this time, enjoying the beauties of his vast estate, which was considerable, as it was one of the largest in Berkshire. He owned farms, houses for rent and even a village.

From here the view was glorious, a vista of trees and lawns with the glint of water in the distance. Far off he could see cottages, their thatched roofs looking cosy and welcoming.

But in his heart he knew that the cheerful appearance was a sham. His estate was in a state of decay because the rents he received were not enough to keep it in good condition. The thatched roofs that looked so fine at a distance were mostly in need of repair.

His own house too required a good deal of work, but

he was too much in debt even to think about it.

Suddenly the brightness of the morning seemed to have darkened. His exhilarated mood of a moment earlier vanished and he began to canter home.

At twenty-eight, good-looking, charming and titled, Francis, Marquis of Wimborton, seemed blessed with life's bounties.

But his existence had become an unremitting fight to raise enough money to keep his estate in good order and he was losing the battle.

Having come into his inheritance when he was only eighteen, he had found it extremely difficult to run and somehow his obligations always outran his income.

Every day it seemed to him he was inundated by requests from people on his estate to help restore their houses, their farms or their stables.

Because he had no wish to admit he was a failure, he had somehow to find the money, even if it was only a little of what they asked of him.

But it simply put him deeper in debt and that debt was growing like a cloud, spoiling the horizon.

He left his horse in the stables and entered the house to be met by his butler with the words,

"Mr. Johnson's here to see you, my Lord."

The Marquis was silent for a moment before he said,

"Show him into the smoking room and tell him I will be with him in a few minutes."

"Very good, my Lord."

When the butler had departed, the Marquis groaned to himself. He guessed why his accountant had come to see him and it certainly would not be good news.

Mr. Johnson was a middle-aged man who had looked after him ever since he inherited the estate.

He was waiting for him as he entered the smoking room.

"Good morning, Johnson," the Marquis greeted him. "I was not expecting you and I hope this surprise visit is not going to be a gloomy one."

He held out his hand as he spoke and Mr. Johnson shook it before he replied.

"I am afraid, as usual, my Lord, I do not bring good news."

"I thought that was too much to ask of you," the Marquis answered with a smile.

He sat down hard in the chair he always occupied. The accountant, whose office was in London and who had therefore made a special journey, sat down opposite him and regarded the Marquis with sympathy.

He had come so young to his responsibilities and Mr. Johnson had thought he would have preferred to stay in London.

Or perhaps he should be abroad enjoying himself with pretty and attractive women, rather than being alone in this huge house and having little to amuse him except the horses and the estate.

To his surprise, however, the Marquis had taken possession of his inheritance when his father died unexpectedly, as if it was not only his duty but a pleasure.

The Marquis smiled at the man opposite. It was not his fault that he had a tale of woe to tell.

With a sigh, Mr. Johnson began to talk. And it was, indeed, a depressing story of mounting debts, inadequate rents, and of problems growing worse every day.

After an hour the Marquis sighed,

"I cannot believe that things are really as bad this."

"I am afraid they are, my Lord, and I can assure you

that I would not have come down from London to upset you unless it was urgent to do something."

"That's all very well," said the Marquis. "I agree with you there is a great deal to be done, especially now that the repairs to this house are three times more than I expected."

"And not only to this house, my Lord. There are at least six houses on the estate which need urgent work, otherwise the tenants may begin to withhold their rent."

The Marquis rose to his feet and walked to the window.

"Why has all this happened so suddenly, Johnson?"

"It's hardly sudden, my Lord. The seeds were planted a long time ago. Your father was told what was required but he, unfortunately, did as little as possible and matters have just grown worse."

"What the devil can I do?" demanded the Marquis.

"I don't want to seem intrusive, my Lord, but have you ever thought, with your title and your position, you might marry an heiress?"

"Marriage!" exclaimed the Marquis. "I've never thought of it chiefly I suppose because I have never fallen in love."

There was silence for a moment and then the accountant said as if talking to himself,

"It seems odd, when you have so many advantages and so many ladies have – shall we say? – expressed an interest, that you have not found even one to suit you."

The Marquis did not reply, but merely smiled as he stood at the window, looking out blindly at the fountain playing in the sunlight.

His success in Society had always been assured. His title had brought him an invitation to every important ball.

Even without the title he would have been in demand,

as he was a true Wimborton, last of a race of tall, broad-shouldered men with handsome looks and dark red hair.

He had inherited these attributes and also a mysterious 'presence', an air of pride in his ancestry and in himself. His appearance in a room was the signal for heads to turn, especially female heads.

Even women who knew nothing of his title could not help smiling at the sight of him, while knowledgeable dowagers hurried to introduce him to the *debutantes*.

He was not conceited, but he had come to take it for granted that he would be welcome anywhere in London Society.

But somehow, although he had danced with the prettiest girls of the year and been invited a dozen times by their parents to luncheon or dinner parties, he had never met a girl with whom he had wanted to spend the rest of his life.

He had in fact found the actresses most amusing who his men friends introduced him to. And, of course, they made him realise how pleasant love-making could be when a brilliant actress melted into his arms and agreed to anything he desired.

But he knew that this was only a passing amusement, which he shared with his friends. After the moment had passed, it was easy to forget until it occurred again.

Standing at the window now he remembered these affairs, so enjoyable at the time, but fleeting pleasure soon forgotten.

Marriage, on the other hand, was something serious, which would last for a lifetime.

At last he sighed and turned back to Mr. Johnson.

"You will think me unreasonable no doubt, but the thought of marrying for money disgusts me."

"I am very, very sorry, my Lord," he replied. "But it

is my duty to tell you the position frankly and at the moment it is extremely bad."

There was silence and then the Marquis said ironically,

"I suppose you have even chosen the woman."

The accountant smiled.

"Indeed I have, my Lord."

"Tell me the worst."

"Miss Lexia Drayton."

The Marquis stared, as Mr. Johnson clearly expected this name to mean something, but he could swear that he had never heard it before.

"I beg your pardon?" he said blankly.

"She and her father moved into Highcliffe Hall last month."

Highcliffe was a large, well-appointed house on the estate and which was in better repair than anywhere else on his property and the Marquis had kept it that way to be sure of securing a tenant who could afford to pay a high rent.

The previous tenant had always paid willingly, delighted with the property, but his wife had died and he had gone to live with his married daughter in Scotland.

It had been a matter of urgency to find a new tenant, but Mr. Johnson had handled it and the Marquis had not yet met Mr. Drayton.

"You were in London when they moved in," Mr. Johnson told him. "I am told that Mr. Drayton is enormously rich, in fact, a millionaire three or four times over."

The Marquis stared at him again.

"On my land? A millionaire?" he exclaimed.

"I understand he has been in America and only arrived in England a month or so ago. He owns a large house in the most fashionable part of London, but wanted a country property.

"Is he English?" enquired the Marquis.

"Yes, he is English," replied Mr. Johnson, "but he went to America and made a fortune there, so much so that he could afford to buy a house in Park Lane and is also purchasing horses at Tattersall's, which he intends to hunt and to race. I understand that Mr. Drayton has only one child – a very attractive daughter, who will inherit his huge fortune."

After a long silence the Marquis muttered,

"So this, you think, is the solution to my problem."

"Why not, my Lord? If he is as rich as everyone says and has only this one child, it seems to me it is a gift from the Gods."

The Marquis laughed.

"Are you really serious? The daughter of a millionaire must have her pick of men."

"I believe she had her pick of them in America, but her father wants an Englishman for her, preferably one with a title."

"I see," smiled the Marquis wryly.

"My Lord, this is no time to be splitting hairs. She has what you need, and you have what her father wants. May I suggest that your Lordship calls on Mr. Drayton as soon as possible, otherwise there are many others who will go knocking at her door. If she cannot win a Marquis she may well settle for something less."

After a pause the Marquis threw back his head laughing,

"I don't believing this is happening! I just don't believe you are standing there having this conversation with me. Are you really saying that a millionaire has chosen to rent one of my houses simply so that his daughter can meet me? It's *incredible*."

"Of course it is, but it's good thinking and I am quite certain that Mr. Drayton has a sharp brain. He wouldn't be a millionaire otherwise."

"But to go to such lengths – "

"It does sound like a play or a novel," admitted Mr. Johnson, "but I was told on good authority that Mr. Drayton has made many enquiries about who was whom."

"It's *too* fantastic for words, but I do want to meet this millionaire. I might persuade him to somehow help me without having to take over his daughter, as though she was a bag of sugar. What did you say his name was?"

"Drayton! Garry Drayton."

The Marquis laughed again.

"The truth is, old friend, you are writing a book and you've made all of this up. Admit it."

"If only I could say that was true, but it is not," responded Mr. Johnson. "But I suppose this might be Chapter One, in which you are the hero, wondering how you can pay your debts and then the perfect opportunity presents itself!"

"I suppose you are relying on Mr. Drayton to pay what would seem a fantastic rent for Highcliffe Hall."

The accountant nodded.

"Your Lordship has never received so much for it before and we'll never get so much from any other tenant if Mr. Drayton leaves, as he undoubtedly will if you refuse to see him."

"All right," agreed the Marquis. "*You win*! I will have a look at this girl, but I assure you of one thing, I have no intention of marrying any woman for her money or for any reason, except for love."

His voice seemed to ring out and his accountant stared at him.

Then unexpectedly he said quietly,

"I admire you for that sentiment, but *needs must when the devil drives*!"

"And the devil is driving now. Damn it! Was any man ever in such an appalling position as I am in at the moment? The sooner we have a drink and try to forget it, the better."

He walked towards the cupboard at the end of the room where his father had always kept his whisky.

As he turned the key and opened the door, Mr. Johnson, watching him, was smiling.

*

At about the same time that the Marquis was riding back to his own stables, another horse was galloping hell-for-leather across the countryside.

From a distance the rider seemed a tall slender lad, controlling the animal magnificently despite his slight build.

A closer view would have revealed that this was no boy at all, but a young woman, unconventionally dressed in a man's shirt and breeches, riding astride.

Her eyes blazed with life and enthusiasm as she soared over one obstacle after another, landing lightly and never losing control of her animal, although he was a large and rather fierce beast.

A little distance behind her rode a middle-aged groom, who finally caught up and addressed her in a beseeching voice.

"You really should stop this, Miss Lexia. The Master will have my hide if he knew you were riding in such a scandalous way."

"No, he won't, Hawkins, because I won't let him. It's all my fault and so I shall tell him, if he ever finds out."

Hawkins's fears were not noticeably soothed by this blithe pronouncement, but he fell silent and cantered after his

Mistress as they returned home.

"Didn't Skylark go wonderfully well this morning?" Lexia Drayton sang out.

"I couldn't say, miss, I was always too far behind to tell," replied her henchman in deep gloom.

Lexia chuckled. She had her own way of doing things and she did not plan to change, even if she raised a few eyebrows.

Just the same, she would rather not have to listen to one of her father's lectures, so she planned to slip into the house by a side door and change into a dress before he noticed her.

It was sheer bad luck that he happened to be looking out of a window as she rode past to the stables.

"Lexia! Come in here at once."

She sighed.

"Yes, Pa."

She jumped down from the huge horse without waiting for assistance, tossed the reins to Hawkins and headed for the French windows that led directly into the breakfast room.

"Whatever do you mean by dressing in such a scandalous way?" her father demanded, coming in from the room next door where he had been watching her. "Go upstairs and change at once – no, on second thoughts, stay here! I have something to say."

"Oh, good, I'm hungry."

She sat down, poured herself a cup of coffee and took some toast, before beginning the task of calming her father down.

"I was only riding, Pa!"

"And don't call me Pa!"

"Why ever not?"

"It's inelegant. English ladies say 'Papa'."

"But I'm American."

"You are not! I am English and your dear Mama was English. You were born in England."

"But when I was three we went to America and I grew up there. I liked it and now I feel American."

"Well, the sooner you stop that the sooner you will be ready to take your place in English Society," said her father firmly.

"Wasn't I in English Society when we were in London?" asked Lexia innocently. "We went to a lot of parties, I remember."

"But you haven't been presented at Court and that is the height of my ambitions for you."

Lexia's eyes twinkled.

"Really? I thought the height of your ambition was to marry me to a great title. The Prince of Wales? Oh, no, I forgot. He's already taken, but he has a couple of sons – "

"Please do not joke about serious matters, Lexia. Why shouldn't you marry the highest eligible man in the land?"

"Because I'm a nobody," she retorted merrily.

"Let me tell you something, my girl. A person with money is never *nobody*. Haven't you learned that yet?"

"I meant that we don't have a title. Not even a little one."

"Your Mama was the daughter of a Knight."

"Yes, but that doesn't impress a Duke or a Marquis. I am a nobody, Papa, and that's fine by me. A happy nobody."

Mr. Drayton stared at her, aghast at such heresy.

"You must not let people hear you say things like that," he scolded in a horrified whisper.

"All right, I won't say them," she said, adding irrepressibly, "I'll just think them."

"Don't even think them. It is time you started behaving like an English lady and adapting yourself to your new life."

"Why can't England adapt itself to me?"

But this idea was so shocking to Mr. Drayton that he could think of no response.

"Never mind that idea," he said at last. "I just don't want to see you throw away your advantages. You were more beautiful than the girls in London and you are more beautiful than any of the girls here."

"Pa!" she exclaimed in mock horror. "You must not say such things as people will think we are rude and offensive. I want the folk around here to like us. I want to go to dances and give dinner parties of our own and I want ours to be the most interesting dinners for miles around."

"From all I hear that won't be too difficult," replied her father. "But this is a very nice County and I too want to be friends with the people who live in it. *Especially the Marquis.*"

There was silence for a moment and then Lexia admitted,

"You talked about the Marquis when we were on our way here and I know that several times you were disappointed that I hadn't met him at parties in London."

Again there was another short silence, while Mr. Drayton seemed to be considering his next words carefully. At last he said,

"He is very important, in fact, one of the most important Noblemen in England."

Lexia gave a teasing laugh.

"Admit it, Pa, you want him to fall in love with me."

"I am making my plans."

"But you cannot plan for people to fall in love. Are

you planning for me to fall in love with him too?"

"He is young and I am told good-looking."

"I am not sure I like good-looking men," responded Lexia impishly. "They are always admiring themselves when I want them to be admiring me."

"He can make you a Marchioness and that should be enough for you."

"But I want to marry someone I love and from all I have heard of English Noblemen – and that is quite a lot – they are very pleased with themselves. In fact, their houses and their wives definitely take second place."

"Why not?" her father asked. "A man should be Master in his own home, but I am determined before I die to see you wearing a really impressive tiara at the Opening of Parliament."

Lexia sighed again. She had heard this all before and she knew that her father was extremely ambitious for her and since he had become so rich he was determined that she should marry one of the nobility.

He had, as she knew, rented this house so that she could meet the aristocracy of England on what they always thought of as their own turf.

Lexia, who had some of her father's brains, knew that he had made enquiries into several Counties before he decided that Berkshire could give him what he required – an unmarried Marquis.

She had tried teasing him about his ambitions,

"Really, Pa, why don't you try to get a title for yourself? I am sure you could become a Duke or even marry the Queen!"

"The Queen is still in mourning for a husband who died thirty years ago. You know, my dear, I am not thinking of myself, but *you*."

"You are thinking of me too much," complained Lexia. "But, like you, I want to live my own life my own way."

Her father looked at her speculatively.

"What does that mean?"

"It means that I will not be pushed into marriage. I intend to choose my own husband, if I must have one at all."

"If you – ? What kind of talk is this? A woman has to marry. It's her destiny."

"Maybe I want a different destiny. You know, Pa, in America I actually met girls who wanted to have a life of their own without being merely an extra wheel on some man's life."

"The sooner you forget that kind of talk the better," he exploded. "I don't know what the world is coming to. Well brought up young women saying such things – "

"Oh, I wasn't well-brought-up," she teased. "Do you know when I was happiest? When we stayed on that ranch in Arizona and I learned to ride bare-back and rope a cow. Gee, that was great!"

"And don't say 'gee'!" he begged. "Where's the decanter? I need a whisky."

"It's too early," she objected. "Lord Eagleton told me that no gentleman drinks whisky in the morning."

"Lord Eagleton doesn't have a daughter who says 'gee' and rides about in breeches," admonished Mr. Drayton with feeling.

"Oh, dear! I am afraid I'm a great trial to you. Poor Pa!"

"Don't call me Pa! Do you understand?"

"Yes, Pa! I mean, no, Pa! *Papa*. Gee, I feel silly saying Papa!"

"And change your clothes into something decent. Ladies do *not* wear trousers."

"I cannot stand the clothes women wear," she protested. "I don't know how anyone can move in them."

"You will never catch a husband dressed like that."

"That suits me!"

"Lexia!" he roared.

"Sorry Pa – Papa. I don't mean to say these things, but they just slip out."

"Didn't your dear mother teach you anything?"

"Yes, she taught me always to be true to myself."

"And being true to yourself means roping and riding on an Arizona ranch, does it?"

"I can think of worse things. She said being true to yourself was the most important thing in the world and she should know because it had worked for her."

"Your Mama said that?"

"She said it was being true to herself that had made her marry you and be so happy with you."

Mr. Drayton was silenced. He was a hard, sometimes ruthless man, but he had loved his wife. It had been his dream to bring her back to England a rich woman and give her the life he felt should have been hers.

But she had died a year ago, just before their return and her memory still saddened him.

"Well, she was right about that," he said. "When I met your mother she was as far above me as the moon and the stars. She was a Knight's daughter and her family wanted her to marry upwards, a Baronet or even a Viscount.

"Then we met. I had just a tiny little business. It was flourishing and prosperous, but her family looked down on me as a tradesmen, so we ran away to be married and her family cut her off and we didn't care. We were happy.

"But it wasn't enough for me. I wanted to be somebody. So we went to America, where I knew I could make a real fortune without anyone bothering about my antecedents. Well, I made it and they won't call me a nobody now. I want you to marry into your mother's world. That's your right and it's what she would have wanted."

Lexia did not answer this directly, but she was not at all sure that he was right. Her mother would have wanted her to marry for love.

She finished her breakfast quickly and went upstairs to put on what her father called, *decent female attire*, and what she called *prison clothes*.

She knew she was treading on dangerous ground in contending with her father. He was very set on having his own way and although she loved him, Lexia knew that he did not want to accept anyone's ideas but his own.

There was bound to be a battle about her marriage, but she was determined to win.

The size of her father's fortune made her suspicious of all men and she had her own ideas of what she wanted.

'I will not marry anyone,' she told herself, 'just to please Papa, even if the man is a King! I want a man who loves me for myself and not my father's money.'

Suddenly she went to her dressing table and from the top drawer she took a tiny photograph, showing a sweet-faced lady with features remarkably like Lexia's own.

It was her mother.

'You would have understood, wouldn't you?' she whispered. 'And if you had been here, you would make sure he understood.'

She sighed and pressed the picture to her breast, murmuring,

'But what am I to do now?'

CHAPTER TWO

The letter came with the early morning post and brought a smile to Mr. Drayton's face.

"It's from Lord Wimborton," he crowed. "At last!"

"You mean, he has finally deigned to notice our existence on the fringe of his glorious orbit?" asked Lexia ironically. "How thrilling!"

"I wish you would not speak like that," scolded her father.

"Well, it makes me furious that you should be so delighted to hear from this man. Who is he? Is he any better than you?"

"He is a *Marquis*," replied Mr. Drayton, as though that explained everything.

"Yes, but is he any better than you?"

"You don't understand. He's a Marquis."

"An impoverished Marquis?"

"Very much so, I believe."

"In that case he *isn't* better than you, he's a lot less, because you didn't sit around on your – "

"*Lexia!*"

" – on your rear end, waiting for a fortune to fall into your lap. You got up and did something about it and that makes you the better man."

"Thank you, my dear. I appreciate the sentiment, even while I deplore the manner in which it is expressed. But I beg you not to say any such thing in front of Lord Wimborton."

"No, he wouldn't want to marry me then, would he?" she grumbled equably. "Could you pass me the toast?"

"With his need for money and the dowry I shall give you, he will marry you whatever you say."

This was an unwise admission as it prompted Lexia to observe,

"Then I can say what I like, since it won't make any difference."

"You will not say what you like," her father fulminated. "You will say what is proper, like any other lady."

"You mean lie?"

"If necessary, yes. Good grief, what did you have an education for?"

"Well, I will probably never meet him anyway."

"You will meet him tomorrow. We are invited to his house."

He read aloud,

"*I feel it is only right to make your acquaintance and to tell you how welcome you are in the County.*

I would like to take this opportunity of inviting you to meet some of your neighbours who, I am certain, will be as willing to welcome you as I am."

"He is going to have all his fine friends in to see if we use the right knife and fork," commented Lexia in disgust.

"You will be there on your best behaviour and looking your finest," ordered Mr. Drayton firmly.

"Yes, Papa."

"That means looking like a lady."

"Yes, Papa!"

"*In a dress*!"

"Yes, Papa."

Lexia escaped before the conversation could go any further, running up to her room and watching from behind the lace curtains until her father had left the house.

"Thank goodness!" she exclaimed. "Now I can go riding."

"Your new velvet habit is most becoming," declared Annie, her maid.

"Velvet habit be blowed! I am wearing breeches."

Annie gave a little scream.

"But your Papa – "

"Would be good'n mad. Why do you think I waited until he had gone? Let's get moving."

The scandalised Annie had no chance to object further as it was useless to argue with Lexia in one of her headstrong moods.

"And you had better send a message to the stables," added Lexia. "I'm riding Skylark and I don't want a side saddle."

Annie dutifully relayed the message, praying not to be around when the Master found out.

At last Lexia was arrayed in riding breeches, boots and a tweed jacket that was comfortable rather than fashionable. Her long hair had been firmly twisted up onto her head and secured by pins and over it she fitted a peaked cap.

With this attire and with her tall slim figure from a distance she could have passed for a boy, which pleased her.

'If only I had been born a boy, life would be so much simpler,' she sighed. 'And more fun!'

In the stables she found Skylark all ready for her, raring to be off, snorting and prancing so that two grooms were barely enough to hold him.

"I wish you wouldn't ride him, miss," implored the Head Groom. "He's dangerous."

"Good!" responded Lexia cheerfully, swinging herself up into the saddle. "That's how I like it."

Seeing her groom about to mount his horse in order to accompany her, she called out,

"No need, Hawkins. I'm riding alone today."

"But miss – "

"Stand clear," she ordered the grooms holding Skylark's head. They obeyed her only too willingly, releasing the reins and dashing clear of the flying hooves.

For the first few miles Lexia gave Skylark his head. He was a powerful animal eager for exercise and he flew over the ground at a speed that exhilarated her.

"Atta boy!" she exclaimed as they finally slowed. "Skylark, you are wonderful!"

Suddenly she realised that nothing looked familiar. She had galloped further than ever before and was now in strange country.

Looking round she thought this was the loveliest place she had ever seen and there was a softness about the greenery that appealed to her.

Just ahead she saw the glint of water where a little stream meandered past and urged Skylark forward, so that he could drink.

He did so gladly and as he dropped his head to the water she noticed the house just up ahead. It was magnificent, made of pale honey coloured stone, and stretching over two hundred yards along the front.

'I wonder if that is where the Marquis lives,' she

mused. 'It's beautiful and I wouldn't mind being invited to a party there or a ball.'

She put her head on one side to consider the house's attributes.

'That terrace looks like the perfect place for a little flirting. You just arrange for your partner to dance you out of the French windows and into the shadows and then – hmm!'

Her lips curved in pleased recollection of balls she had attended in the past, the young men who had been only too glad to flirt with her and some enchanting moments in the shadows.

But she also realised something else.

'It would take a pile of money to keep up,' she murmured to herself. 'So this Marquis thinks he's going to make himself a fortune through me. And if Pa has his way, he will.'

She considered this thought for a moment.

'I don't think so,' she said to herself at last. 'Not even for *that* house.' "C'mon, boy."

She patted Skylark and turned to start the ride back.

After a while she became aware that someone was behind her.

Looking back she saw a shabbily dressed man on horseback, waving and calling to her.

"Hey you, boy! Come here!"

'Oh, goodness!' she muttered. 'That's all I need, someone who's seen me dressed like this. If Pa hears about it, he'll never let me forget it.'

She urged Skylark faster and he responded at once. Now she was doing what she loved and everything else fell away again in the joy of riding a really fast horse.

From behind her she could hear the man shouting

angrily and she thought she heard the word 'trespass', but it was hard to be sure.

'And I am not waiting around to find out,' she thought grimly, spurring Skylark on to greater efforts.

The thought of being trapped by one of the Marquis's grooms and perhaps hauled in front of his Lordship was distinctly unpleasant.

Even if she escaped that fate there was still the chance of being recognised and reported to the Marquis as a hoyden, a young woman who did not know how to behave like a lady.

Not that she cared what he thought of her! She had no intention of being handed over to him in marriage.

But she wanted the refusal to be on her side, not his. To be rejected as 'not quite the thing' would be a hideous fate.

The man shouted again and she looked behind her, finding to her dismay that he was gaining on her.

Occupied thus, she failed to notice the tree trunk across her path and when Skylark soared across it, she was unprepared.

The sudden movement upward shifted her to one side so that she lost her balance and the next moment she was flying through the air.

The world seemed to spin wildly until at last the earth came up to meet her with a thump that nearly knocked all the breath out of her.

She lay there on her back, breathing hard, while everything settled back into place. Then the man and his horse came soaring over the tree trunk, heading directly for her.

"*Whoa*!" she yelled, rolling sharply to one side just in time to avoid the flying hooves and covering her head with her arms.

The horse landed, turned and halted. The man dismounted and came towards her, dropping to one knee.

"Are you all right?" he enquired coolly.

"I think so – no thanks to you," Lexia snapped.

"It seems to me that you have come by your just deserts," he said. "There is no right of way across this land."

"I was only taking a ride."

"In a place where you have no right to be. Let it be a lesson to you, young fellow. Come on, up with you!"

"Take your hands off me," she raged as he reached for her.

His answer was to seize her arms and haul her to her feet.

Outraged at this disrespectful treatment, Lexia lashed out with her feet and then, after managing to get one arm free, with a hand.

"That's enough!" the man roared.

Lexia's answer was another swipe, which he narrowly dodged. Exasperated she stamped her foot and was rewarded by a yell of pain.

"I said that's enough!" he yelled.

"Oh, no, it – isn't," she gasped, flailing furiously.

"That's it, young fellow," growled the man through gritted teeth.

Taking her by the shoulders, he gave her a shake, not hard enough to hurt her, but hard enough to dislodge her peaked cap, which went flying off.

The next moment her long fair hair cascaded around her shoulders and the man was staring at her in dismay.

"You're a girl!" he exclaimed.

Lexia could have screamed with vexation. This was the worst thing that could have happened.

"Yes, I'm a girl," she replied gruffly.

"Dressed like that?"

"Oh, for pity's sake!" she exploded. "How would you like to ride a side saddle and wear a dress?"

A slow grin crept over his face.

"Well, if you put it that way, I don't think it would suit me," he agreed.

There was something about his smile that was irresistible, she discovered. In fact, he was a handsome man, tall, broad-shouldered and with dark red hair.

She allowed herself a moment to regard him with pleasure. She had not known that servants were so good-looking in this County.

She had, as yet, no ear for the nuances of English accents or it might have occurred to her that his voice was too cultivated for a servant's, despite his clothes having seen better days.

So there was nothing to suggest to her that this might be the Marquis himself.

"Definitely not for me," he repeated, "but then, I am not a lady."

"Neither am I, according to Pa," grumbled Lexia. "And now I've gone and made a mess of everything."

He stared at her baffled.

"What have you made a mess of?"

"Well, it's – it's sort of a long story."

"In that case you had better tell me in comfort. Why don't we make our way over there to the lake?"

The way led through a little clump of trees, which crowded down to the edge of the water. There the horses drank gratefully and Lexia dropped to her knees to bathe her face in the deliciously cool water.

When she had finished she went to join him on a tree stump where he was sitting, moving carefully because she was still sore from her landing.

"Are you hurt?" he asked. "You took a nasty tumble."

She shrugged.

"That's nothing. I've had worse."

"So if that isn't what is troubling you, what is it?"

She sighed.

"It's the Marquis."

"I beg your pardon!" he queried, startled.

"The Marquis. You know, the one who owns this place? Warburton – Wilberry – ?"

"Wimborton," he said.

"Are you sure? I was certain it was Warburton."

"I assure you, he is the Marquis of *Wimborton*."

"Oh, well, I expect you would know, wouldn't you?"

"I expect I would," he agreed gravely.

"Have you worked for him long?"

"Have I – ?"

"Well, that doesn't really matter, but you do know him? I mean, you could pick him out of a crowd?"

"I think I could manage to do that. But how does he come into this?"

"Well you see – it's really all his fault," Lexia told him distractedly.

"Good Heavens! What has the poor fellow done?"

"Don't call him poor fellow," said Lexia darkly. "He's a terrible man. I hate and despise him."

Her companion stared for a moment, but then recovered himself and managed to speak with composure.

"Have you known him for long?"

"I've never met him."

"But even so you know him to be hateful and despicable? That's quite a burden for any man."

"He wouldn't care."

"If he knew he had incurred the censure of a lady who hadn't even met him I think he would care about that."

"Why should he? He must have women swooning at his feet and ready to let him get away with anything that he likes, just because of his title."

Her companion opened his mouth to protest about this unjust assessment, but the realisation that there was a hint of truth in it held him silent.

"Sometimes – perhaps," he said carefully. "But that doesn't mean it's what he likes."

"He doesn't *think* he likes it, but he's used to it," Lexia pointed out. "He knows nothing else, so of course he expects it. He is Lord of all he surveys and he thinks he only has to snap his fingers and people will come running."

"But that still doesn't explain what he has done to incur your dislike," the man parried, carefully not answering this last remark.

"He has put me in an impossible position. At least, Pa's done that, I suppose. But he wouldn't have done it if it hadn't been for this Marquis, so it's his fault too."

Her companion rubbed a hand over his eyes.

"I seem to be unusually stupid today, but I must confess myself totally at a loss. Why are you in an impossible position and what does the Marquis have to do with it?"

She gave him a sharp look.

"You did say you knew him, didn't you?"

"I – er – yes," he floundered.

"He must never know. Oh, please, promise you won't

tell him. Pa would never let me hear the end of it."

"It's all right," he assured her. "His Lordship and I don't discuss such matters. I won't tell him – whatever it is you don't want me to tell him. What is it, by the way?"

"That you found me dressed like this."

"I promise not to tell him, but why is it significant?"

"Because I am supposed to marry him."

After this there was a silence.

"*What*?" he managed to say at last.

"Pa's set his heart on him marrying me. It's a tomfool idea because I don't suppose he wants me any more than I want him, but I can't talk sense to Pa."

A strange look had come over the man's face.

"Just – who – is your father?"

"Garry Drayton. We are renting Highcliffe House."

"Garry Drayton, hmm! Would he be the – er –millionaire?"

"You have heard of him?"

"I think everyone in the locality has heard of him. Myself, I don't believe most of the stories. I have never heard of anyone who actually possessed a million pounds."

"Oh, Pa has more," she said indifferently. "He made it in the California gold fields."

"California," he murmured.

"In America – that's where I've lived for the last eighteen years."

That explained her voice, he thought. He had been trying to place her accent.

"By the way, I am Lexia Drayton."

She extended her hand, giving him a friendly smile. He seemed nonplussed and she realised that she had offended against some social code. It probably wasn't 'the done thing' to shake hands with a servant.

Then he offered his own hand.

"My name is Francis."

"Francis. Do people call you Frank?"

Again there was the brief hesitation, as though she had caught him off-guard.

"Nobody ever has before," he admitted truthfully. "But please call me Frank, if you wish."

"Thank you." Then she sighed. "Oh, Frank, it's terrible!"

"Terrible to be a millionaire?" he echoed.

"Dreadful!" she confided. "They all want to marry me for Pa's money."

"And what do you want?" he asked sympathetically.

"I want to avoid the Marquis. I don't want to be frog-marched up the aisle to find him standing there waiting for me, gloating over the prospect of getting his greedy hands on Pa's money."

"So you think he's desperate to marry you?"

"Not *me*, the money. They say he's in a bad way and he'll do anything for hard cash."

"Do they, indeed?"

"But I don't want to marry a man who thinks he's some little tinpot King. He probably does all sorts of feudal things like – like shooting peasants before breakfast."

There was a stunned silence.

"Why would he do that?" asked Frank at last.

"Because he's their Liege Lord and – and the peasants work for him, and if he isn't pleased with their work – he shoots them!"

"But this is the nineteenth century. Your ideas are about six centuries out of date. I promise you that he hasn't shot a peasant in years – not before breakfast anyway."

"Are you sure?"

"He isn't allowed to any more."

She gave him a suspicious look.

"You're making fun of me."

"Well, maybe just a little," he agreed wryly.

"But you really do promise not to tell him that you saw me like this in these clothes, riding without my groom? It would make him look down his nose at me."

"But, if it turns him against you – isn't that what you want? Maybe it would put him off marrying you."

"With *my* money and *his* problems? I don't think so!"

"You think he's so desperate that he will marry you anyway, even looking down his nose at you?"

"Some men will do anything for money," confided Lexia darkly. "But I don't want him thinking I'm not a lady – even if I'm not."

Frank's lips twitched.

"So you don't really mind if he falls at your feet, but only so that you can grind him beneath your heel?"

"That is overstating the case," she came back stiffly.

"Of course, I can see why you would want to receive his proposal, even if you don't mean to accept it?"

"You *can*?"

"If he's as desperate for money as you say, but didn't propose, it would amount to saying that you are so far beyond the pale that even your father's money cannot make you acceptable."

Lexia stared at him, speechless with indignation, while he warmed to his theme.

"Naturally you would not want that, especially after your father appears to have made his ambitions fairly plain.

For an heiress to set her cap at a Marquis is bad enough. For her to do so and fail would be mortifying beyond belief."

"Hey, you!" she cried, outraged. "I haven't set my cap at anyone."

"No, but it's being done on your behalf and you will get the blame."

"I – I – "

"And you are not being very fair to the Marquis. You claim the right to hate and despise him, but he must admire you."

"You're on his side, aren't you?" she challenged.

"I must admit I am."

"Yes, well, if you work for him, I suppose you have to be," admitted Lexia, trying to be fair.

"True, but I can sympathise with your problem. You need to bring him to the point where he's eager to marry you, but will not make a nuisance of himself when you reject him."

"That's right! But if I receive a proposal Pa will expect me to accept. And if I don't, he'll throw himself into a rage."

"I feel reasonably certain that you will know how to deal with your father."

"I hope you're right."

"Anyway, this is all in the future. You might never meet the Marquis."

"I am going to meet him tomorrow. We've been invited for tea so that he can look me over."

"That will be your chance to astound him by your beauty, grace and wit. Wear your finest clothes and don't let him lord it over you."

"I certainly won't let him do that."

"Your pride is at stake and you can snub him later."

"Well – I don't wish actually to wound him."

"That would be impossible," said Frank solemnly. "His heart is too armoured to feel a wound."

"Really?"

"I have to admit the truth. He is everything you have said and worse. Proud, arrogant, thinking himself above the world."

"That's disgraceful!"

"He thinks every woman he meets is after his title. He will disdain you from the first moment."

"The cad!"

"You must teach him a much needed lesson. Your unfortunate situation is clearly his fault and he should be made to suffer."

"It will be a pleasure to do so," she vowed.

He rose, holding out his hand to draw her to her feet.

"I am obliged to you, sir, for your good advice."

"You are welcome to all I can do for you."

She clasped his hand, smiling and saying,

"If I ride this way the day after tomorrow, perhaps we will meet again."

He smiled.

"I feel fairly sure that we will. Goodbye – for the moment."

*

Nobody dared to tell Mr. Drayton about his daughter's ride and he remained in happy ignorance.

Next day it was a pleasure to him to see how diligently Lexia prepared for her meeting with the Marquis. He had feared that her rebellious mood might spoil her chances.

Instead to his great satisfaction, she spent the morning 'primping herself' as he put it.

This involved an hour in a scented bath, followed by another hour choosing the correct attire.

It was a difficult choice with subtle nuances. To appear at her best, without seeming as though she was putting herself out to attract him, was a task that might have taxed the skills of King Solomon.

At last Lexia and Annie settled on a supremely elegant gown of greyish-green silk, tight at the waist and flared at the hem. Tiny flowerets of green velvet adorned the front.

The hat which completed this outfit was green straw with a grey ribbon and small black plumes at the back.

It took another hour before Annie had achieved the perfect hair style on which this hat should sit. When she had finished, all Lexia's beautiful fair hair was swept up onto the top and sides of her head.

Finally, the important choice of jewellery. One perfect pearl glowed against the cravat and two matching pearls adorned her ears. They were simple, but fabulously costly.

Annie handed her a parasol of green silk trimmed with lace.

Now she looked as she wanted to look. Magnificent. Splendid. A woman who was not to be trifled with.

Her father was waiting for her as she descended the stairs into the hall.

"Excellent," he purred. "You look just as I had hoped."

"I am glad that you feel I do you credit, Papa," she said demurely.

"You would do any man credit," he declared. "Come, my dear! Let us go out and conquer the world."

CHAPTER THREE

"You look so lovely," her father told Alexia as the carriage bowled along. "I think any man would fall at your feet."

"I am not going to listen to you," she replied firmly. "I want to enjoy the sunshine and the beauty of the countryside and not think of having to marry a man who I haven't even met and who doubtless will look down on us."

Her father stiffened and she knew he was going to make a violent response, so to prevent him from doing so she slipped her hand into his.

"I love you, Pa, and I want you to be happy. But you will find that women are more difficult to move about than pounds and shillings, so you must give me plenty of time before I make up my mind."

He did not answer and she added coaxingly,

"And I am *not* in a hurry to leave you."

She knew by the way her father looked her that he was touched and she felt his fingers tighten against hers.

"You are very sweet, my darling," he muttered gruffly. "You must forgive me if I seem in too much hurry, but I do want you to be happy and I want you to have everything you want in life."

Lexia smiled and then she lifted his hand and kissed it.

"I do love you, Pa," she sighed, "but you of all people must realise that each of us has to fight for what we think is right for us. So do not be too harsh on me. Give me time to breathe and find my own destiny and don't forget, I am your daughter, which means I have to think for myself, just as you have always done."

Her father chuckled.

"That's true. I remember my father saying to me, 'you will do as I tell you,' but I thought, I'm damned if I will and I did not!"

Lexia laughed too.

"Well, if *I* said, 'I'm damned if I will,' you might be displeased with me."

"I certainly would."

"But I will say that I have a lot of you in my blood, so I have to do what *I* think is right, as well as what *you* think is right."

Her father laughed again.

"I love you too, my dearest," he said, "and I am very proud to have such a clever daughter. It is only natural that you should want some freedom of choice. I am not a tyrant."

They drove on in silence, but Lexia knew that her father had understood only a part of what she had said. Despite everything he still believed he could arrange matters so that she would choose the Marquis.

She had freedom of choice – as long as she chose according to his wishes. And that was no freedom at all.

'And he doesn't know what I know about the Marquis,' she thought, remembering what Frank had told her that afternoon.

'*Proud, arrogant, thinking himself above the world.*'

But at least she had been warned, thanks to Frank, who had already been a good friend to her. She would now pursue her own strategy – to make him fall at her feet, while not falling at his.

And perhaps she would see Frank tomorrow, tell him how matters had gone and receive his further advice.

The thought of meeting him again brought a smile to her lips. He had been, she recalled, extremely good-looking.

Closing her eyes, she summoned up his face again, the dominant nose, the firm chin, the dark hair with a touch of red.

His mouth too she remembered very clearly. It had been wide and generous, a mouth made for kissing.

Then she checked herself. Frank was a servant, an employee on the Marquis's estate. She pictured her father's reaction if he could read her thoughts and shuddered.

But an independent spirit made her say,

"You know, Pa – Papa, I learned many lessons in America and one of them was the idea that all men are equals."

"The sooner you drive that nonsense out of your head, the better!"

"But is it nonsense? Suppose I was to choose a really fine man, who didn't have a title?"

He turned his head to stare at her, aghast.

"*What did you say?*"

"I want to fall in love as you fell in love with Mama. Whether a man is a Duke or a road-sweeper what matters is whether I love him or not."

Her father breathed hard.

"If you think you are going to throw yourself and my money away on a nonentity, you are very much mistaken."

Lexia sighed.

"Yes, Papa!"

"Let me tell you one thing, my girl. Whatever people say about equality, I have discovered that the top of the world is much more comfortable than the bottom. And don't you ever forget it."

"No, Papa."

"I had thought we settled all this last time we talked."

"Last time we – ?"

"You know who I am talking about," said Mr. Drayton darkly.

Since she had no idea who he was talking about, Lexia could only gaze at him blankly, which made him say,

"Don't give me that innocent look, my girl. Wayne Freeman, that's who it is! You should have got over him by now."

"Wayne – ?" echoed Lexia.

She had met him at a ball in New York, about six months ago and liked him. Wayne was a big, booming young man with a heart of gold and nobody could have called him sophisticated, but he had the charm of a boisterous puppy and Lexia had enjoyed his company.

In fact she had enjoyed it so much that her father had become worried and declared he would never allow her to marry him.

But Wayne had never once proposed and she would not have accepted anyway. He was more like a big brother who she was very fond of and it was exactly because he was not trying to wheedle her into marriage that she found his company pleasant.

But her father could not believe this and lectured her endlessly about 'giving him up'. It was about that time that he had begun to hint about coming back to England.

"You would not have been happy with him," he returned to the fray now.

"Pa, I never – "

"He was just a rough diamond."

"And what, pray, is wrong with a rough diamond?"

"Nothing, in its place – "

"But you don't think his place is with your daughter?" she challenged, her anger flaring in defence of her friend.

"Not going up the aisle, no," her father asserted firmly.

"Really! Well, let me tell you that Wayne Freeman is a good man, a man any woman would be proud to love – "

"I told you to forget him," snapped her father. "Now, you do as you are told and *forget him*. I won't let you marry him and that's final."

"Rather him than this horrible Marquis, any day," she snapped back.

"That's enough. I don't want to hear another word. I did the right thing in bringing you home and it seems I did it just in time."

Lexia subsided, seething and wishing she had controlled her temper a little better.

Fond as she was of Wayne, she had not the least desire to marry him. A more subtle man than Mr. Drayton would have realised as much, but he had blundered on, annoying her until she leapt to Wayne's defence.

Now he was more convinced than ever that she had lost her heart to her American friend, but that might be useful, she realised, in the coming battle about the Marquis.

So she said no more and began to look out for the Marquis's house, for she was sure she recognised some of the scenery she had seen the day before.

Suddenly the carriage turned a corner, the trees seemed to part and there was the great honey-coloured building glowing softly in the sun.

It looked even more beautiful than she remembered

from yesterday and she gazed at it entranced.

In America she had become used to everything being large, huge buildings and great distances. Now she saw grandeur and she thrilled to it.

Then she remembered that to have the house she would have to accept the dreadful Marquis and decided that she would do without the house after all.

Now they were on the last stretch, heading for the front door and Lexia had a sudden feeling that everything was going too fast.

There were nearly at the front door and she felt a sudden conviction that she was going into danger.

If she were wise she would make some excuse to keep away, but now it was too late, as the horses drew up outside the front door.

It was already standing open and she saw there was a butler waiting for them and two footmen wearing very smart uniforms.

'Please God, help me,' she prayed in her heart.

Her father gave their names to the butler, who inclined his head and led them through the front door into the Great Hall.

"I will inform his Lordship of your arrival," he intoned and sailed loftily away.

Mr. Drayton looked around him at the hall with its huge staircase rising up for three floors. Lexia heard him give a sigh of contentment and knew what he was thinking.

It was certainly magnificent, but she could see that work needed to be done. The wallpaper was in poor condition and so was the paintwork, but beneath the shabbiness there were still the remains of splendour.

The walls were covered with pictures, climbing up to the ceiling. There were ladies in ruffs and farthingales and men in embroidered satin coats and knee breeches. Some of them wore the powdered wigs of the eighteenth century, while others showed their natural hair, a dark red.

Looking at that hair, Lexia felt the first stirring of uneasiness.

Then she noticed that the features of all these men had a remarkable similarity. The wide generous mouth that told one story, the stubborn chin that told another, the glint in the dark eyes that told a story of its own – these features were common to all of them.

And she had seen them before.

"Who is this man?" she casually asked one of the footmen.

"That, miss, is Francis Bernard Charles Wickham, the fourth Marquis."

"And the man next to him?"

"Francis Michael Andrew Wickham, the fifth Marquis."

"Another Francis?" she queried.

"It is a family name, miss. The heir to the title is always called Francis."

"Indeed?"

She tried to speak normally, but the word almost choked her.

But she still fought not to believe it. English aristocrats were notorious for seducing the local maidens. Everyone knew that and the family face could probably be found all over the district.

And if his mother had called him Francis? That meant nothing.

So she argued valiantly with herself. Anything was better than the monstrous suspicion that was plaguing her.

It was impossible.

Simply impossible.

It *had* to be impossible!

She went on telling herself that right up to the moment that the Marquis of Wimborton advanced down the hall to greet them.

And it was Frank.

He was dressed differently now in an elegant grey frock coat with an impeccable cravat.

But it was undoubtedly Frank.

"Mr. Drayton," he said, holding out his hand in welcome, "it is a pleasure to meet you at last."

"Good afternoon, my Lord. We are delighted to be here and I have been admiring your great house all the way up the drive."

"I am very proud of it myself," replied the Marquis pleasantly.

"May I introduce my daughter, Lexia?"

"Enchanted," muttered the Marquis bowing.

Out of the corner of his eye he saw that a footman was relieving Mr. Drayton of his hat. Taking advantage of his guest's momentary distraction, he enclosed Lexia's hand in both his own.

"I have been anticipating our meeting," he said in a low voice, "with great interest."

She took a deep breath.

"I'll bet my bottom dollar, you have!" she seethed.

"Bet your bottom dollar?" he echoed, wrinkling his forehead. "I have never heard that said before."

"You've never met anyone like me before," she informed him in the same soft furious tone.

"I have no doubt of it. I take it the expression is American?"

"It certainly is and I have a few other choice examples for you."

"How charming!"

"I am not feeling charming right this minute," she snapped.

"No, I dare say you are feeling very angry with me."

"Angry doesn't begin to describe it! If I said I would like to boil you in oil, you might begin to get the general idea!"

He smiled ruefully.

"I think I realised that before you said it."

"Good. Then we understand each other."

"But that's just the point, isn't it?" he asked. "We *do* understand each other – much better than if we had met in the normal way."

"I have nothing further to say to you," she fumed.

"That's just as well, because your father is beginning to stare at us. Shall we go into the drawing room and you can meet some relatives of mine?"

He ushered them into the next room, where two little old ladies sat. At the sight of the newcomers they looked up, bright-eyed with pleasure and expectation.

"This is my Aunt Letitia and this is my Aunt Imelda."

In fact, as the ladies hastened to explain, they were really his great-aunts, the sisters of his grandfather. They lived somewhere in the great house.

"I'd be lost without them," the Marquis said warmly. "As long as they are here, I am not living alone."

The old ladies beamed at him contentedly.

Lexia guessed that they too were as poor as the church mice that they resembled and would have had no refuge if he had not allowed them to live in the nooks and crannies of his home.

It was Lexia's first experience of a great English country house. Highcliffe was nothing compared to it. Here the high rooms, the ornate ceilings and the gilded chandeliers made her feel as though she was stepping onto another planet.

At first all she saw was the splendour, but then she noticed that the curtains were threadbare, the ceilings needed cleaning and so did the carpet. The wall-paper ought to be renewed and the chandeliers regilded.

Tea was served in the drawing room and Lexia realised that the tea set was the best Dresden china. But there were only two cups to match the teapot and the other three were all different, although still Dresden.

The ladies were overwhelmed at meeting someone who had actually come from America, which they appeared to believe was on the other side of the moon.

They bombarded Mr. Drayton with questions and he gave them all his attention, either from kindness of heart or because he wished to win the Marquis's good opinion and knew how to do so.

Whatever the answer, he raised no objection when the Marquis suggested taking Lexia away to show her the house.

Lexia rose and followed the Marquis from the room, declining, however, to take his arm.

"You are still angry with me?" he enquired.

"That surprises you?"

"I had hoped that the opportunity for reflection would have presented matters to you in a happier light."

When she declined to reply he continued,

"May I congratulate you on your appearance, ma'am? It is everything I had hoped and you have no idea how it pleases me to see my advice taken."

Remembering how he had advised her to dress and why, Lexia turned on him, cheeks flaming.

"You are insufferable! How dare you speak to me like this?"

"I merely complimented you on your gown."

"Do not play the innocent with me, sir. You are reminding me of the utterly disgraceful things you said to me yesterday afternoon."

"I seem to recall making some very rude remarks about myself – remarks that I am sure you now agree with."

"I think no fate is bad enough for you," she choked.

"So you said yesterday. In fact now I think of it, I was almost as uncomplimentary about myself as you were. Hatred and scorn were the kindest emotions you expressed about me."

Memories of her own incautious behaviour flooded her, making her uncomfortable, but she carried on straight into the attack.

"You should surely have told me who you were immediately," she declared.

"What and miss hearing so many fascinating comments about myself? That is asking too much."

"You did not behave like a gentleman."

"And you did not behave like a lady. Which is excellent. Just think of what a lot of time we could have saved. Without yesterday we might never have known the truth about each other."

"I am certainly glad to know the truth about *you*," she countered stiffly.

"Precisely. Just think how disgracefully I might have imposed on you. As it is, when you see the shocking state of my house, you will know why our marriage has even been contemplated. You have been forewarned, ma'am. I am a heartless fortune hunter and no woman should have anything to do with me."

She eyed him grimly, appreciating the humorous turn he had given the situation, but unwilling to relent too soon.

"In fact," he sighed, "the more I think of it, the more I feel you should be grateful to me for exposing the ugly truth about myself to an innocent lady, who might otherwise have been deluded."

"I am not that easily deluded," she told him firmly.

He gave her a hilarious look.

"Except by unscrupulous persons who conceal their true identity," she added hastily.

"But I *am* an unscrupulous person."

"You certainly are," she said, thinking how insufferable it was of him to accuse himself before she could do so.

"Exactly what I said, ma'am."

"You behaved unspeakably, encouraging me to put out lures to attract you – "

"Only so that you could have the pleasure of grinding me to dust, ma'am."

"Which I could never have done, because you were armoured in advance."

Memories were whirling about her head now. One, in particular, made her want to scream with shame and vexation. He had said –

"*You think he's so desperate that he'll marry you anyway, even looking down his nose at you?*"

And what had she replied? Something about him being prepared to do anything for money.

Oh, how could she have said that? How could he have duped her so easily?

How could she wreak her revenge?

"I tell you frankly, sir," she said now, "if there is one thing I regret more than any other, it is that I will not have the pleasure of grinding you to dust."

"Beneath your heel?"

"Beneath both my heels."

"You were especially looking forward to that, I gather?"

"Definitely!"

"Perhaps I could suggest some other method of entertaining you?"

"Nothing will compensate me for that loss."

"There is always revenge," he suggested.

This accorded so well with her own thoughts that she was too startled to reply.

"As I show you round my dilapidated house, you will have the pleasure of seeing how badly I stand in need of your money. Picture to yourself my bitter regret that I have forever put it out of my own power to woo you into – er – handing it over."

Lexia lips twitched.

"Yes. I think I shall enjoy that thought."

She had to admit that the condition of the house was shocking. In the ballroom she saw that the ceiling needed repair and the pictures needed reframing.

The music room as well was in a disgraceful state.

"I have been unable to do anything to this room," the Marquis was saying. "In fact, I seldom come into it, as it depresses me. As you know anything as old as this house requires thousands of pounds to bring it back into what it was in the past."

He sighed.

"Quite frankly it is impossible for me to find so much money, so I shall have to marry an heiress. Do you happen to know any?"

Lexia's struggled to suppress a smile. It was harder to dislike the Marquis than she had thought.

"Heiresses do not grow on trees, sir."

"I am sadly aware of that. The only heiress of my acquaintance is an awkward creature who would certainly knock me to the floor with her parasol were I to attempt to make advances."

"Then be warned and do not."

"I shall heed your warning, ma'am."

"Besides there must be many heiresses on the catch for you."

"For my title, ma'am, only for my title. It's a melancholy thought."

"Yes, it is," she agreed instantly. "Do you ever see people looking in your direction and realise suddenly that they are not looking at you, but at something beyond you?"

He nodded. "I see it all the time. It's rather like being a ghost."

"Yes, and you want to call out and remind them that you are actually there."

They looked at each other in mutual sympathy.

"They don't understand," said Lexia at last. "Nobody understands what it's like."

"Except us."

"Yes, except us."

They walked on their way through the great house, feeling more at ease with one another.

CHAPTER FOUR

When the tour of the house was over, the Marquis with Lexia on his arm descended the stairs and approached the drawing room. At about the same moment each began to slow down, as though reluctant to go any further.

"I wonder if we are thinking the same thought," murmured the Marquis.

"They will stare at us as we enter the room," replied Lexia.

"Yes, they will," he agreed. "And they will speculate."

"They will smile to themselves."

"And each other."

"It doesn't matter how blank we keep our faces," she added desperately.

"They will read into them whatever they want to."

Just in front of the door they stopped.

"Perhaps we could quarrel," she suggested hopefully.

He shook his head.

"They will interpret it as a lovers' tiff. Whatever we do, they will believe what they wish."

"You mean it's hopeless?"

"No," he asserted in a decided tone. "We will defeat them."

"How?"

"By standing together."

"Shoulder to shoulder."

"Side by side."

They faced the door. She slipped her hand into his arm and they advanced together.

Their entrance was as awkward as they had feared. Mr. Drayton and the two ladies glanced up quickly before looking away, trying to seem uninterested.

The Marquis handed Lexia to her seat and offered her some tea, which she accepted politely.

The air was tense and then to their relief, the butler entered.

"Lady Overton, my Lord."

The Marquis looked up in surprise as through the doorway came a middle-aged woman whom Lexia thought must have been very pretty when she was young.

She was dressed in sensible country clothes and could never have been anything else but an Englishwoman.

"Dear Francis, I thought you might be at home," she gushed as she sailed across the room. "I wanted to tell you that we are having a party next Wednesday and I have the most attractive people coming whom I know you will enjoy. So don't tell me you are too busy to come."

"Of course not," answered the Marquis. "Any party of yours is always amusing."

"I have some special guests from France, whom I am sure you will love to meet," she told him.

Then as if she had only just noticed them, she stared first at Lexia and next at her father.

"I don't think you have met my guests," said the Marquis. "They have just returned from America and have moved into Highcliffe Hall."

Lady Overton held out her hand to Mr. Drayton.

"I am delighted you are here," she cooed. "In fact I have been complaining for ages that we never have any interesting new people in the County. The last tenant of Highcliffe Hall lived a very solitary life."

Abruptly she switched her attention to Lexia, looking her up and down with eyes that were sharp and full of curiosity.

"My daughter, Lexia," Mr. Drayton told her.

"So you are the lady I have heard so much about," exclaimed Lady Overton. "My dear, the whole County is talking about you. How wonderful to meet you at last."

She shook hands with Lexia, while her eyes continued to bore into her.

Lexia had seen that look before and secretly relished it. It meant that the newcomer was assessing her, trying to decide whether she represented a threat to long-cherished plans.

And Lexia did represent a threat. She knew it and the other woman knew it as well, and the smile she gave Lady Overton was implicit with the knowledge they both shared.

Lady Overton's smile wavered only slightly.

"We need new people here," she continued, "and I am sure you will help us to make Berkshire far more exciting than it is at the moment."

"We are really looking forward to joining in the life of the County," replied Lexia politely. "But, of course, as we have only arrived recently, we know very few people."

"You will know no one better than Francis," Lady Overton rambled on. "He is the person who can make things quite brilliant and when he is not around everything is deadly dull."

"Now you are flattering me," came in the Marquis.

"No, it is the truth! I will be very upset if you do not come to my party because my dear sister, Martha, is coming down from London especially."

She looked at the Marquis in a provocative manner as she carried on,

"You know how she loves dancing with you and I am determined we will have the best band available, so that the evening will be a success even before it begins."

"All your evenings are successful and I will look forward to seeing Martha again."

At this Lady Overton simpered and could not resist taking a sideways look at Lexia to make sure that she had understood the significance of *Martha*.

"Now that Mr. Drayton has taken over the house," Lady Overton resumed, "we will expect him to provide us with new parties, new ideas and of course, young people."

Lexia realised that her father was enjoying this conversation. He seemed unable to understand that Lady Overton was patronising him.

"I promise you," he said, "that I will make Highcliffe Hall a riot of fun and gaiety, but, of course, having been away from England for so long, I will need your help as to whom I should invite."

Lady Overton laughed and responded at once,

"I can see you have all the right ideas and, of course, I will be only too willing to help you."

She gave another simper at Lexia, as she added,

"And I am sure the young men will welcome your pretty daughter with open arms."

'You hope they will,' thought Lexia, amused. 'Thus leaving Martha a clear field with the Marquis.'

"I will be grateful for any help you can give me," Mr. Drayton confirmed.

"My pleasure," purred Lady Overton. "Now I simply must rush away. "Francis, *dear,* you haven't forgotten that I am expecting you for dinner tomorrow night. It will be just a small party, a few of our most *intimate* friends and I know I can depend on you."

The Marquis hesitated and Lexia thought she understood why. For Lady Overton to mention this dinner party in front of the Draytons, while so pointedly excluding them, was an act of rudeness and it had embarrassed him.

She waited with interest to see what he would do next.

At last the Marquis spoke.

"As a matter of fact, Honoria, I fear I shall be unable to come to your dinner, much as I was looking forward to it."

"Oh, but why," she demanded petulantly.

"Mr. Drayton has been kind enough to invite me to his house tomorrow evening."

"But I am sure he will understand that you have a prior engagement – " Lady Overton began to protest.

"Indeed he would, since he is all kindness and generosity, but as he and his daughter are newcomers in the district, as well as my newest tenants, I feel they are entitled to every courtesy. I am certain that you would feel the same."

There was a pause while Lady Overton regained her composure and hoisted her smile back into place.

"But of course," she concurred. "In fact – " she seemed to have been struck by sudden inspiration, " – why should not Mr. Drayton and his daughter come to my dinner party tomorrow? Then the whole district can welcome them."

"An excellent idea," agreed the Marquis affably.

"Your Ladyship is too kind," accepted Mr. Drayton quickly before she could change her mind.

She regarded him with disfavour.

"Yes, well, I am sure we can squeeze in two more without too many problems. You are very welcome, of course. Well, I must be going. It's all going to be so lively at Overton Park!"

She paused to added significantly,

"My young sister Martha is coming from London very soon, a *fascinating* beauty."

She was still talking as she walked towards the door.

As the Marquis opened it for her she said in what he imagined was meant to be a whisper, but which was easily heard by the others in the room,

"Martha is just longing to meet you again. She has such blissful memories of the last time you danced together."

Then she was gone.

"Honoria does tend to be a little over-powering," explained the Marquis. "But she means well. Sir, I apologise for claiming an appointment with you tomorrow without your consent – "

"No apology is necessary," said Mr. Drayton graciously. "You were too kind."

"Then it is agreed that we will all attend the party together? I will call for you at six o'clock."

Mr. Drayton left the house in seventh heaven. All the way home he talked about the evening to come and in his mind he was already half way to his goal.

"Don't take so much for granted, Papa," Lexia warned him. "There is always Martha and I think Lady Overton is making plans."

"Pooh, whoever Martha is, if he was going to marry her, he would have done so by now. No, my dear, he is yours for the taking."

"Papa!" she exclaimed and then corrected herself with

a warning look at their coachman's back.

"Nonsense! A well-trained coachman forgets what he has heard as soon as he's heard it and Jack is very well-trained."

*

If the Marquis had one true friend in the world it was his valet, Jenkins.

He was a calm unhurried man in his fifties, who had been with his employer for fifteen years and was devoted to him.

The Marquis trusted him completely and when he was preparing for bed that night he felt able to confide in him. He was surprised to find Jenkins in a sombre mood.

"I need hardly say, my Lord, that all your tenants and dependents are hoping to see you make a match with this lady. Everyone would be simply delighted."

"Everyone except the lady herself," added the Marquis wryly.

"Unfortunately, my Lord, that is true," said Jenkins with a deep sigh.

The Marquis stared.

"What do you know about it?"

"I know, my Lord, that the lady *loves another.*"

He uttered the last words in a portentous tone that left no doubt that they were highly significant.

"Considering the depth of the lady's feelings, sir, I fear it may be very hard for you to make any headway."

"Jenkins, what are you talking about? Who says that she loves another?"

"The lady herself says so, my Lord."

"To you?"

"No, to her father. Jack, their coachman, is courting

my niece, Sally, who is your second under-housemaid. While he was here this afternoon he went to the kitchen and they got talking. Being a good girl, she felt obliged to inform me of what he had said. Apparently Miss Drayton and her father had the most terrible scene in the carriage on the way here."

"About this man she loves?"

"Yes, my Lord. His name is Mr. Wayne Freeman and he is an American gentleman. Apparently Miss Lexia is wildly in love with him, so much so that Mr. Drayton was forced to leave America to take her away from this man's influence."

"Great Heavens!"

"He has forbidden her ever to think of him again, my Lord."

"But she cannot forget him?" asked the Marquis in a hollow voice.

"It seems not, my Lord."

"She actually declared her love for this man?" he asked cautiously.

"Apparently, my Lord, the lady flew into a great passion, wept and stormed and declared that she would marry him or die."

"I see. That will be all, Jenkins."

"Goodnight, my Lord."

The valet bowed himself out.

Left alone, the Marquis turned out the light and sat for a long time in the darkness, brooding over what he had just heard.

He was not acquainted with Sally, so he had no idea of her love of romantic melodrama, nor had he allowed for the wild exaggeration that Jack would naturally employ in seeking to win and keep Sally's attention.

At last he walked to stand in the window, looking out over the moonlit gardens, a prey to deep thought.

*

The next morning he rode out to the place by the water where they had talked. He was not quite sure what he was expecting, but when he saw her riding towards him he knew that he would have been disappointed if she had not come.

She saw him from a distance and waved.

She was in breeches again, riding astride, her hair swept up and hidden under a peaked cap.

He too was dressed in the rough clothes he had worn at their first meeting.

He took a moment to admire her riding and the way she controlled a great brute of a horse with only the lightest movements.

Then he turned his horse towards her and cantered ahead, pointing to his right, where there was a way over clear ground. She nodded and turned in the same direction.

He joined her and for a while they galloped side by side, gathering speed on the powerful beasts that they both rode harder and harder.

He found that she was a match for him. She feared nothing, whether it was the highest fence or the widest ditch and if he increased his speed, so did she, daring him.

It was exhilarating to be with her.

At last they slowed and brought their horses to a halt.

"Thank goodness!" exclaimed Lexia. "Now I feel I can breathe again."

"Did you know I would be waiting for you?"

"Not exactly know, but I hoped you would. If you only knew how badly I need someone to talk to!"

"But I do know, it's the same with me."

"If you could have heard my father. He didn't stop talking all last evening and now he has met you, he thinks you're wonderful."

"I hope you told him I wasn't."

"I tried, but it was hard to be convincing after you were so nice to us. That made it very difficult for me."

"I beg pardon, ma'am," he said meekly. "I'll try to do better next time."

They found a stream and dismounted to allow the horses to drink.

"Does you father know you are out here, dressed like this?" he asked, laughing.

"I told him I was going riding with the Marquis, so he didn't raise any objection. But the truth is that I came to meet my friend, Frank."

He grinned.

"You are not still angry with him, then?"

"I cannot afford to be," she replied simply. "He's the only real friend I have. Besides," she added, with a smile, "he is my spy in the camp."

"Ah! You mean he can alert you to how the Marquis's mind is working?"

"Exactly. So I hope he has plenty of information for me now. How were things after we left yesterday afternoon?"

"The ladies were delighted with you. They said so to his Lordship at length and repeatedly."

"That must have made matters very difficult for him."

The Marquis smiled.

"He is not averse to hearing you praised, ma'am, especially as his own view of you was entirely favourable."

"That is kind of him when I am making his life so

difficult. I actually feel rather sorry for the Marquis, being badgered to marry when he doesn't want to."

"He copes with it fairly well," the Marquis told her. "Don't forget that he has been raised to think of marriage as a duty he must one day perform for the good of his estate."

"But what woman wants to know that a man has married her for duty? What kind of marriage could they have? How would she look at him and what would she expect to see in his eyes?"

She gave a heavy sigh.

"And what *would* she see in his eyes? Weariness and resignation, the knowledge of a life that might have been so much happier."

He nodded.

"The Marquis feels the same. You see, he has always cherished the notion that somewhere in the world is a woman who will love him for himself alone – without thinking of the worldly advantages that he can bring.

"And he hoped that if he was patient he would find that woman. But time passes and she seems to slip beyond his grasp."

"I know just how he feels," said Lexia earnestly. "It's what we all want, isn't it – someone who prizes us for ourselves. Oh, Frank, if we are not careful, they will marry us off to each other before we know what's happening."

"No, they won't, I won't let it happen."

"I have said that to myself, but, although I might try to stand up to my father, I don't know how much success I would have. It's so much easier for a man to be strong. So if you are as determined to avoid our marriage as I am, then I feel there is hope."

He looked at her strangely.

"But hope for what? Hope that one day you may be

reunited with the man you love?"

Lexia glanced at him quickly.

"I know," he told her. "I know about Wayne Freeman."

"But how – ?"

"Servants' gossip. Forgive me for heeding it, but I am glad to know the truth."

"I wonder what, exactly, you think is the truth?" she enquired cautiously.

"That you love this man and your father forced you to leave America to take you away from him."

"It wasn't quite like that – "

"Please – " he held up a hand to stop her. "I am not prying into your private affairs. I have no right to do so, but I merely feel ashamed of some of the things I said to you when we first met. When I think that I actually implied that you were setting your cap at me – well, I don't know how to look you in the face."

Since this imputation had been the one that annoyed Lexia the most, she found a certain amount of pleasure in this moment. She had no desire to deceive him, but she was glad to have him realise that she was *not* setting her cap at him.

After a moment she said carefully,

"You will understand that this is something I cannot discuss."

"I would not for the world intrude upon your most delicate feelings," he assured her. "But may I ask – do you really despair of marrying him?"

"I would never be so poor spirited as to indulge in despair," she riposted firmly.

"Of course not. You are all courage, but do you not still cherish the dream of being united with the man you love?"

"Please," she said hurriedly, "do not speak of him as the man I love – "

"Forgive me, that was tactless. I only meant – I am too much your friend to want to stand between you and your happiness."

"You do not, I assure you. There is no question of our marriage."

"You think your father will remain intransigent?"

"I am convinced of it. Besides, I don't even know where Wayne is."

"Didn't you leave him behind in America?"

"He left New York to go off on his travels. He may still be there or he may have come to Europe."

"In search of you?"

"No, not looking for me," answered Lexia quickly.

She was finding it difficult to talk about Wayne in the face of the Marquis's conviction that they were in love.

"You must not think of me as broken-hearted," she told him, meaning only to be honest. "I do not dream of marrying Wayne."

"I admire you for refusing to wear your heart on your sleeve. You mean that your father has crushed your dreams. Obviously this man cannot help you climb the social ladder that is so important to him?"

"He has nothing to recommend him but a good heart," smiled Lexia, "and he dances very well."

"A poor recommendation in a husband."

"Now you sound like my Papa."

"Don't say that. Believe me truly to be your friend. Is there nothing I can do to help you?"

Lexia laughed.

"You can protect me from the others."

"Yes, I can do that and you, in your turn, can protect me."

"From Martha?"

It was a shot in the dark.

"Yes, from Martha. I promise you, I could really do with your assistance there."

Lexia gave him a look of mischievous innocence.

"But I understood from Lady Overton that you and Martha are practically engaged."

He threw her a dark look that made her giggle.

"Is she not a great beauty?"

"Indeed she is. Every feature is fine and perfectly formed."

"But her purse is not large enough?"

"She is well-dowered, beautiful, elegant and virtuous," the Marquis told her, speaking like a man reciting a lesson.

Lexia stared, willing him to go on.

"But I could not make myself marry her," he confessed at last.

"What fault do you have to find with her?"

"None, that is what terrifies me. Her voice is low and well-modulated, she never says anything out of place – "

"Not like me?"

"Definitely not like you. Her behaviour is definitely ladylike. She would never have ridden out without a groom."

"A paragon of virtue?"

"A bore," he said gloomily. "Whatever is there, is perfect, but so much is missing. When I am in her company I never feel that I dare laugh too often."

"Good Heavens! How terrible! Then I promise to

look after you."

"My dearest friend!"

He clasped her hand warmly and she clasped his back.

"You are going to be on show at Lady Overton's dinner tonight," he warned. "The neighbourhood will be there, getting your measure."

"Then I must not disappoint them," she enthused, her eyes gleaming with pleasure.

"Remember," he told he, "*be magnificent.*"

Lexia laughed.

"But that was for yesterday."

"Tomorrow night you need to be even more splendid – for Lady Overton and the whole neighbourhood."

"Very well. Magnificent."

He held her horse's head while she mounted.

"Until tonight," he murmured.

"Until tonight."

CHAPTER FIVE

True to his word, the Marquis arrived at six o'clock that evening.

Lexia descended the main staircase to find him waiting in the hall below with her father and they looked up to watch her with differing degrees of satisfaction.

Mr. Drayton nearly burst with pride at the picture his daughter presented. She was wearing a dress that she had bought in London and which had originally been imported from Paris.

The Marquis also regarded her with pleasure, although his was quieter and more restrained. He thought she looked exquisitely beautiful and would surely outshine all the ladies at the dinner party.

He wondered if Wayne Freeman truly appreciated what he had won and why he had allowed himself to be frightened off – the ungrateful dog!

The Marquis knew that if he had won such a prize as this woman he would have allowed no man to frighten *him* away.

It seemed that Lexia was like so many women who gave their hearts to men who were unworthy of them.

For a moment this thought made the Marquis feel a little savage, but there was no sign of anger in his eyes as he stepped forward to take her hand and lead her down from the last step. His eyes were filled with smiling admiration.

The sight comforted Lexia. This was not the terrible Marquis being driven to pursue her for gain.

This was her friend Frank.

"My compliments, madam," he began lightly. "You look – " his eyes teased her, "*magnificent.*"

She smiled at him understanding his joke.

Mr. Drayton watched them in seventh heaven. Already he could hear wedding bells.

His joy was increased when he saw the Marquis's carriage displaying the Wimborton coat of arms on the panels. All his efforts in London had not enabled him to arrive at a party in this kind of style.

For the entire journey he beamed at the other two sitting opposite him in a manner that made them both feel self-conscious.

It was twilight when they reached the Overton mansion, which was flooded with lights. As the carriage drew up outside, two powdered footmen advanced to open the door and let down the steps.

The Marquis offered his arm to Lexia and indicated for Mr. Drayton to go ahead of them, an act of courtesy that pleased Lexia, but strained Lady Overton's sense of etiquette.

She was forced to greet Mr. Drayton effusively first, before turning her attention to the man who was her prey.

Even then it was hard for her to keep smiling at the sight of Lexia on his arm, but she still had her trump card to play, so she bided her time.

For a while she contented herself with introducing the Draytons to her other guests, every one of whom knew in advance about the huge Drayton fortune – Lady Overton had made certain of that.

She had also invited several young men to meet them, all of whom crowded around Lexia.

Lexia understood perfectly. She had been through this ritual many times before and she knew how to play her part with ease. Also some of the young men were extremely good-looking, so she decided to enjoy the evening.

"Isn't she charming?" Lady Overton cooed to the Marquis. "So unspoiled! So rustic!"

"So rich!" murmured the Marquis, appreciating these tactics. "Lord Charles, the Honourable Ferdinand, the Honourable Augustus and Viscount Frain. All of them in need of cash. You are playing a deep game, Honoria."

"I am merely introducing her to likely prospects."

"You may think them likely, but her father won't."

"But she might. Charles is so handsome."

"He is also practically half-witted and let me assure you, Honoria, that the lady has all her wits about her."

Since this was precisely what Lady Overton was afraid of, she decided it was time to play her ace.

"And now I have the most wonderful surprise for you," she gushed. "Who did you least expect to see tonight?"

"I really could not say," the Marquis responded politely, while an uneasy feeling began to grow in the pit of his stomach.

"Oh, I am sure you must guess. She turned up *so* unexpectedly and we were all *so* thrilled. I told her to stay out of sight at first and not spoil the surprise, but *here she is*".

Following her pointing hand the Marquis turned his appalled gaze to the staircase, at the top of which stood Martha.

Lexia saw her too and regarded her with interest. Martha was undoubtedly the most beautiful young woman she had ever seen, but there was a cold perfection about her that reminded Lexia of a marble statue.

She was dressed in a ravishing gown of white silk and tulle with pearls around her neck and in her ears.

In fact, she looked like a bride.

She evidently commanded general admiration for the young men gathered at the foot of the staircase to watch her descent. But none of them moved forward to greet her. They all knew that she was hunting very big game.

The Marquis knew it too, but good manners obliged him to step forward and take her hand, greeting her pleasantly.

Lexia could not help observing how well they went together. His height and air of distinction perfectly matched Martha's flawless porcelain beauty.

Nature had meant her to be a great lady, Lexia thought. Possibly a Marchioness and from the way she took the Marquis's hand, it was clear that she thought so too.

Then Lady Overton was ushering them all into the dining room, showing Lexia to her seat, between Lord Charles and Viscount Frain. The Marquis naturally was next to Martha.

This was the kind of situation, Lexia mused, where he felt as hunted and miserable as she did herself. She sent him a look of sympathy, but instead of returning it, he seemed content to devote himself to Martha.

Which left her nothing to do but flirt with the two young men on either side of her and a third who smiled at her across the table. Seeing that there was no better way of passing the evening, she concentrated on enjoying herself.

Luckily Viscount Frain was a wit and her merry laughter frequently rang out down the table. Occasionally this would make the Marquis glance at her with a little frown, but his attention was soon reclaimed by Martha's elegant hand on his arm.

After that Lexia did not glance in his direction again.

Lady Overton was looking insufferably smug.

Mr. Drayton was glowering. He was not a subtle man, but he could read the atmosphere where his own interests were concerned.

Lady Overton beamed in Lexia's direction.

"It is so delightful for us to meet new people," she proclaimed. "I fear that in our little corner of the County we are becoming sadly out of touch. Miss Drayton and her father come from another part of the world."

There were smiles all around the table.

"Of course, my dear," Lady Overton droned on, "we understand that things are done differently over there, so you need not be shy if you find everything a little strange."

Lexia was silent for a brief moment. Lady Overton was patronising her and it was like a declaration of war.

She raised her head at last and if the Marquis was the only person at the table who recognised that she had accepted the challenge, to him at least the glint in her eye was perfectly clear.

"You mean if I don't use the right knife and fork?" asked Lexia sweetly.

Lady Overton's smile became glassy and around the table there were a few intakes of breath.

"I am sure we would all like to hear about High Society in America," she said.

"I couldn't tell you about that," replied Lexia affably. "I preferred cowpunching myself."

Her accent, which had become more English recently, had reverted to American and a slightly theatrical bluntness had crept into her manner.

Her father noticed it and glared.

The Marquis noticed it too and watched her with increased interest.

Beside her Lord Charles gave an inane giggle.

"Cowpunching?" he echoed. "You punch cows? With your fists? I say, doesn't it make them frightfully annoyed?"

"It does a little," agreed Lexia, through quivering lips.

"There's a machine," came in the Marquis, sounding as though he was speaking with difficulty. "It punches a hole in the cow's ear so that it can be tagged for identification."

"I say! How frightfully – frightfully – oh, I say!"

"Very interesting!" observed Lady Overton coldly. "I thought we would have a little dance later. Nothing formal. We will push back the carpet and enjoy ourselves."

She might call it informal, but she had managed to secure the services of a six piece orchestra.

With only thirty guests, there was a restricted choice of partners, which was, perhaps, what Lady Overton had intended.

The Marquis danced with Martha while Lexia juggled with admirers. But he was a gentleman of perfect manners and all his hostess's efforts could not make him dance with Martha a second time until he had taken the floor with Lexia.

"I want another dance too," he murmured as he swept her into the waltz. "And another after that."

"More than two is hardly proper," she reminded him.

"To blazes with that!" he exploded, forgetting for a moment that he was a gentleman. "If you don't help me they'll have me primed for slaughter before the night is out."

"I thought you seemed very happy in her company."

"Only as much as politeness required. At least I was not flirting outrageously with her."

His tone made Lexia look at him sharply.

"What do you mean, 'flirting outrageously'?"

"I would have thought my meaning was all too plain."

"Are you accusing me of flirting with someone."

"Not with 'someone'. With three all at once."

"How dare you! I may have done a little flirting, but I was certainly not outrageous."

"I call it outrageous when a woman claims three men simultaneously."

"I did not claim them. They pursued *me*."

Something seemed to have annoyed him for he could not resist saying in a grumpy tone,

"Which you knew very well how to make them do."

"You are mistaken, my Lord," Lexia informed him with dangerous sweetness. "I have never yet had to *make* a man come after me. They just do."

"In crowds presumably?"

"Oh, yes, they always come in crowds."

He glared at her.

"Oh, be reasonable!" she said, exasperated with him. "I had to do something after Lady Overton practically poked me in the eye with Martha. If you think I am wearing the willow for you – "

"I have not asked you to do so," he pointed out stiffly.

"You expect me to sit there like a wallflower while you shower attentions on the woman who is destined to be your bride – "

"I do not intend her for my bride – "

"But Lady Overton does and I think she's probably a better fighter than you."

"You underestimate me, madam."

"And *you* underestimate her. How do you think Martha got here? She wasn't due for days."

"I have been wondering about that myself," he admitted. "She told me she suddenly took it into her head to start her visit a few days early."

"What a coincidence!"

"Don't you believe it?"

"Do you?"

"No, I think Lady Overton sent her a telegram. If she sent it yesterday, after she left your house, there would be plenty of time for Martha to arrive today. Lady Overton had to do something once she had discovered the threat."

"Threat?"

"Don't try to be modest. You know as well as I do that you are the biggest threat the matchmaking Mamas of this region have seen in a decade. I feel I ought to apologise for the way she behaved at dinner, but you dealt with her so well."

Lexia laughed.

"I've faced worse than her."

"Perhaps Lady Overton should be careful."

The music was coming to an end and Lord Charles was hovering to make sure nobody snatched Lexia from him.

Lady Overton and Martha were also hovering, their smiles like glass.

When there was a pause in the dancing for the guests to get their breath, Mr. Drayton appeared at his daughter's elbow.

"You handled that badly," he growled.

"Handled what badly?" she asked innocently.

"I saw you dancing with him."

"Isn't that what you wanted?"

"You weren't supposed to quarrel with him. Don't deny it. I could see you and I even heard you say, 'how dare you!'"

"I was annoyed."

"You should have concealed it."

"You say that without asking why I was annoyed with him."

"Surely I don't have to explain that the Marquis is a great man and a certain latitude must be allowed him."

Lexia blinked.

"What are you saying?"

"If he made – er – suggestions that you might have considered improper – that is, if he allowed himself to – well, you get nowhere by becoming hysterical. You should have controlled your annoyance."

Lexia stared at her father.

"Pa, are you saying that I should have allowed him to misbehave?"

"Only a little bit, my dear."

"Well, you cannot misbehave very much in the middle of a dance floor," she observed.

"Exactly. You were protected by your surroundings and I am not saying that you should forget that you are a lady, but there's no need to be prudish."

"Prudish! *You* call me prudish and *he* complained that I was flirting outrageously at the table."

"So you were," agreed her father instantly. "I was most shocked by the freedom of your manners. I thought those young men went beyond the line."

"But you just told me I could allow a man to misbehave, as long as it wasn't too much," she pointed out.

Her father breathed hard.

"I was talking, as you very well knew, about the Marquis. Don't pretend to be stupid, Lexia."

She faced him, her eyes glinting.

"Pa, have you ever considered the appalling possibility that I really *am* stupid?"

He glowered and left her.

She danced with the Viscount, then Lord Charles, then the Honourable Ferdinand. Before Lord Charles could claim her again the Marquis stepped in.

"Dance with me," he insisted firmly, "before I lose my sanity."

But they had only danced a few steps before he seized her hand and marched out of the French windows.

"What are you doing?" she demanded, running to keep up with him. "People will talk about us."

"Let them. It may stop them trying to marry me off to Martha. You have no idea what I am going through."

"Of course I have. Do you know what my father said to me tonight? He said that if you – you know – tried to – "

"Take liberties?"

"Yes. According to him I should let you. It's all part of trying to snare you, you see. I mustn't be prudish in case that puts you off. Did you ever hear such stuff?"

She was seething with fury.

"It makes sense from his point of view," observed the Marquis mildly. "If I was to compromise you, I would have to marry you. That's what he's thinking."

"Well, you're not going to compromise me," she snapped.

"I might be held to have done so by dragging you out here."

"Oh, nobody will notice"

"On the contrary. They are watching us now. Look."

He pointed back the way they had come through the trees. An interested little crowd had gathered in the French windows.

"Your father, Lady Overton, Martha," he murmured. "It's time for action."

Before she knew what he intended, his arm was about her waist.

"What are you doing?" she gasped.

"Compromising you – just a little."

As he spoke he was drawing her against him. Lexia had the strange feeling that all the breath had deserted her body.

"Is this wise?" she mumbled.

"As long as we look convincing without – "

He too seemed to be having trouble with his breathing.

Lexia could feel the imprint of his fingers against her waist and the warmth of his body against hers and the sensation was unnerving.

"Laugh," he whispered. "Let them know that my company fills you with delight."

Lexia immediately gave vent to a merry peal of laughter and he responded in kind, looking down into her face with a beaming smile.

"Let us pause by this tree for a moment," he said, leaning against the trunk. "Put your hands on my shoulders."

She did so, looking up directly into his eyes and feeling the world spin.

"Don't worry," he told her in a shaking voice. "I am not going to kiss you."

"You're – not?"

"I promise. I am a man of my word. Don't you believe me, Lexia? *Lexia?*"

She came out of a dream.

"What did you say?" she muttered.

"Do you believe that I'll keep my word and not take advantage of you?"

"Yes," she said reluctantly. "I do."

"Just enough to save me from Martha. I wouldn't ask it of any friend but you."

As he spoke softly his warm breath whispered past her face, making it hard for her to think, but she pulled herself together and managed to speak in a teasing voice.

"Be careful or you might really have to marry me."

"Heaven forbid!" he responded with feeling. "You would turn me white-haired in a month."

"You are surely not suggesting that I am worse than Martha?"

He seemed to consider.

"I would say the two of you were neck-and-neck. Ouch! My ankle!"

"You deserved that," chuckled Lexia.

She was feeling pleasantly light-headed.

"You're not supposed to kick me," he complained. "It spoils the picture we are trying to present.

"Don't worry, I only kicked you very discreetly on the side they cannot see."

He took a deep breath.

"I think we should go back now," he suggested.

"We've given them all enough to talk about."

"Have we? Are you sure?"

"Any more and you *will* be compromised."

For a wild moment she was on the edge of saying, 'what does that matter?' Then she wondered at herself for straying so close to disaster and forced herself back to reality.

73

"We must certainly avoid you compromising me," she pointed out. "That would be stepping from one disaster into another."

"You are a very wise woman."

Arm in arm they made their way back to the house, where, as he had said, a little crowd was watching them.

Lady Overton was looking daggers and Martha was looking sulky, whilst Mr. Drayton was looking as though all his dreams had come true at once.

Soon after that he declared that his daughter was feeling weary, which was the signal for the Marquis to announce their departure and the evening was generally felt to be at an end.

On the journey home Mr. Drayton preened himself, smirked and asked pointed questions about their 'little walk' until Lexia wanted to die of shame.

"And you, Papa," she asked, pointedly trying to change the subject. "Did you enjoy the evening?"

"Oh, what do I matter, as long as you had a nice time, my darling? And I can see that you did. Of course it was a little unconventional of the two of you to go off alone, but I am sure that in the circumstances – "

He paused in a clear invitation to them to announce 'circumstances' that included an engagement. Neither of them replied.

He tried again.

"Of course I wouldn't dream of asking what you were talking about. Certain conversations should remain private until – until a suitable time – "

"His Lordship was trying to make me feel a little easier about the way Lady Overton patronised me at dinner," said Lexia.

In only, she thought, her father would be silent, while

she struggled to come to terms with her thoughts.

What had happened in the garden had shaken her.

She and Frank were friends. They had said so and friends help each other and in his moment of crisis he had turned to her for help and she was glad about that.

If only she could forget the feeling of being pressed against his hard body, his breath whispering against her face, the disturbing glint in his eyes.

But she would forget about it soon, she told herself. She would work hard at it, but it was hard to do so when she was seated opposite him – they had both resisted Mr. Drayton's attempts to seat them together – giving her a warm reassuring smile.

"I thought Lexia stood up for herself very well," commented the Marquis valiantly. "By the way, sir, did you see Lord Overton's smoking room? I believe – "

He continued talking, diverting Mr. Drayton away from the dangerous subject. In this vein he managed to keep the conversation neutral until they reached Highcliffe Hall.

The Marquis bade them goodnight and continued on his way.

Lexia hurried to bed, knowing that she could not endure questions from her father that night.

*

Next morning the Marquis was waiting in their usual place and after a while the sound of hoof beats made him look up.

He saw what he had expected – Lexia, in breeches, riding hell-for-leather in his direction. He rose, smiling and went to meet her.

But she was not smiling as she threw herself from the horse's back so fast that she staggered and he had onto hold her.

"I have only a little time," she said breathlessly. "I came to say goodbye."

"Goodbye? But where are you going?"

"Anywhere!" she cried. "Anywhere away from my father. I cannot endure it a moment longer."

"I understand how you feel but – "

"You don't. You cannot understand how desperate I feel to be harassed and badgered all the time."

"Is this because of last night?" he asked gently.

"Last night was terrible, *terrible*. I wanted to die of shame at the way he behaved."

"Yes, I saw that he was embarrassing you on the way home, but surely, if we can enjoy it as a joke together – "

"I cannot make a joke of it any more," she shouted. "He is trying to sell my life and it is *not* for sale."

She brushed aside the tears of anger and desperation.

"Of course it isn't," he tried to soothe her. "You know I will help you stand up to him."

"But what about afterwards? When he loses hope in you, there'll be someone else. You won't always be there to help me and there is only one answer. I have to escape now, *now*!"

Her tears would no longer be held back and she burst into violent sobs.

The Marquis wasted no more time on words, but gathered her comfortingly into his arms, so that her head rested on his shoulder.

"Don't cry," he tried to calm her. "We'll find a way."

"There's only one way," she wept. "I have to run away. I *have* to."

"But my dear girl, you cannot just dash off on your own like that. You could run into all sorts of dangers."

"I don't care!" she cried passionately.

"But you soon would care. I cannot let you do this."

"You can't stop me."

"I think I could. In fact I think it's my duty to stop you running into danger."

"It has nothing to do with you."

He gave her a little shake.

"Lexia, please try to be sensible. Come over here and we will talk about it and see what can be done."

He led her firmly over to the tree stump, made her sit down and sat down beside her.

"Now dry your eyes and we can look at this problem in a practical way."

"It's hopeless," mumbled Lexia miserably.

"What a girl you are! One minute saying that nobody's going to stop you and the next minute, saying it's hopeless. It isn't hopeless while I am here, because I am your friend. Lexia, please believe me, I will do anything to help you. Anything at all."

"I know you mean well, but you cannot really help," said Lexia despondently, "because there's nothing you can do – unless – *unless* – "

Her face brightened. In a moment a smile transformed her.

"What is it?" he asked her with deep foreboding. "Lexia, tell me what terrible idea you have just thought of. Unless what – ?"

"Unless you come with me."

CHAPTER SIX

For a long moment he did not answer her. From the way he was looking at Lexia he might have been struggling to believe his ears.

At last he found his voice.

"*Unless I* –?"

"You said I couldn't do it alone and you are right, but suppose we both went away together."

"Lexia – "

"We could be brother and sister. Just two ordinary English people travelling together."

"Travelling where?" he asked in alarm.

"Anywhere! The whole world lies before us."

"You mean – travel abroad? That's a completely mad idea."

"Why?"

"Well, for one thing I have no money. Have you forgotten that I am a pauper?"

"But I'm not. I could pay for everything because Pa has always put lots of money into the bank for me in case I wanted it, but since he also pays my dress bills directly I have never needed money until now."

Abruptly his face darkened.

"Let *you* pay for *me*?" he echoed aghast. "Are you

seriously suggesting that I live off you?"

"Well, if you don't have any money and I have some, it makes sense."

"I am not just talking about travel expenses. There is also the question of my creditors and if I just vanish they will think the worst and bankrupt me."

"Not if you give them some money before you go."

"I don't have any money. If I had, I wouldn't be in this mess. Or are you proposing to pay that too?"

"Of course."

"Lexia," he growled dangerously, "do you know what kind of man lives off a woman?"

"Yes. A poor one."

"That is *not* amusing."

"I am not feeling very amused either. It's only two minutes since you said you would do anything I asked. Anything at all you said and what happens the minute I ask for something?"

"But I never thought of anything as mad as like this wild idea."

"It doesn't matter. I'll go alone."

He tore his hair.

"I have told you already it's too dangerous."

"But you would rather leave me in danger than sacrifice a little pride to help me," she accused him.

He gaped at her.

"Of all the shocking arguments – you ought to be ashamed of yourself trying to back me into a corner like that."

"You need not give the matter another thought."

"I – I – Lexia really you shouldn't be allowed out. You are dangerous."

"Does that mean that you will?" she asked, correctly interpreting his tone.

"I – no – I will not do this, *I will not do it*!"

"I understand," she said mournfully. "It's my problem, not yours."

"*All right*!" he roared. "I'll do it."

There was a silence.

"Do you mean it?" she enquired in a small voice.

He looked at her exasperated.

"I have to do it, don't I?" he said. "Because I don't want your dreadful fate on my conscience."

Lexia gave a little cry.

"Oh, do let us do it while we have the chance," she pleaded. "We may never have the chance again."

The Marquis smiled.

"We will be brother and sister, but even so, we cannot go completely alone for the sake of your reputation. I will bring my man, Hawkins, and you must bring a maid."

Lexia was thinking fast.

"I will go home for the money and give it to Annie, my maid. Send your man over to the oak tree just before the entrance to the drive and Annie will give it to him.

"If we do it today, will you have time to make all your arrangements with your creditors, so that we can leave tomorrow?"

"I am sure I can, but – " he rubbed his eyes. "I still feel I ought to refuse this madness."

"Frank, don't you understand? If we give in now and let them force us to marry, neither of us will ever be happy again. We will always be thinking that we have missed something wonderful that has gone for ever, but this way we will each have a chance to find the person we are really destined to love and be happy with."

He nodded.

"You are right. Now tell me what we will do."

"I am going to leave that to you," replied Lexia. "You are a man and you can arrange for us to travel on a ship and we will have to creep out of the house early in the morning so as not to be seen and stopped."

The Marquis resigned himself to his fate, but felt compelled to add,

"But if everything fails and we come home disillusioned and despondent, I swear that somehow I will pay back your money back."

"We are going to win," answered Lexia positively. "I am absolutely sure that if we search ardently for what we believe is true and wonderful, we will find it. *I am convinced we will find it*!"

She pulled a rueful face.

"But we will have to be very careful," she added, "because everyone will try to stop us."

"I should rather think they might," he declared with feeling.

"You make all the arrangements, Frank, then I will be ready exactly at the time you tell me and we will just disappear."

"If we fail, we fail!" sighed the Marquis, "but at least we will have done our best and we will have no one to blame but ourselves."

*

For Lexia the rest of the day was filled with tension.

First she had to arrange her departure with Annie.

"I cannot go without you, Annie," she pleaded.

"Of course you can't, miss," replied a shocked Annie.

She folded her arms and looked forbidding. She was in her thirties and the best maid Mr. Drayton had been able to hire to transform Lexia into the perfect English lady.

They had been together for three months, but in that short time Annie had become devoted to her Mistress and partly this was because she had never before had such promising raw material to work with. Lexia's beauty, her tall elegant figure and her shining blonde hair were a challenge to her skills.

"But my father must not know anything until we have left," explained Lexia.

Annie was wide-eyed.

"You mean we're running away, miss?"

"Yes. It will be very difficult."

"It'll be fun," trilled Annie with an ecstatic sigh. There had been very little fun in her life.

"Then let's get to work. The first item we need to arrange is money."

She had told the Marquis she had money her father had given her, but had omitted to mention that she had no bank account and therefore kept it all in her room.

There was a box beneath her bed and she and Annie hauled it out together and rummaged through it until they reached a large envelope at the bottom.

"Take this," she told Annie, separating out two thousand pounds and putting the rest back into the envelope. "Go to the oak tree at the entrance to the drive and wait for a man called Hawkins. And be careful."

Annie gasped.

"Oh, yes, miss. I'll dart from tree to tree and look over my shoulder – "

"There's no need to go that far. Just try to look normal."

"Do we know anything about this man Hawkins?"

"He is the Marquis's valet."

"Oh, miss, you mustn't do that. He'll tell him we're going."

"He already knows and he's coming with us!"

"But – "

While Annie was still trying to work this out Lexia urged her out of the door and began work sorting out her clothes.

After an hour Annie returned to report that she had encountered Hawkins, had not been impressed with him, but had duly handed over the money and received a note in return.

Eagerly Lexia opened the note and read,

"*Your father is spending tomorrow with the Master of the Hunt. A carriage will call for you at noon and it would be wise not to keep it waiting.*"

There was no beginning or end, but Lexia thought the Marquis was being discreet.

As they began packing the clothes Annie asked,

"What are you going to tell Mr. Drayton, miss?"

Lexia sighed.

"I shall have to tell him that I am visiting friends. I don't like deceiving him, but the way he keeps badgering me leaves me no choice."

"But will he believe you have vanished just like that?"

"Strange as it sounds, I think he will, because the truth will never occur to him."

But she knew the letter to her father would have to be very carefully worded and at last she sat down to write it.

She said she knew that he would understand that she wanted to have a look round before she finally made up her mind to do what he wanted. And where could be better than to look in London?

"*We have so many friends in London,*" she wrote, "*and I know they will be pleased to see me.*

If I go from one to another I will not be in any way tiresome. All the time I will be able to meet gentlemen I did not meet the first time I was in London. I am sure that one of them at any rate will meet with your approval."

She thought as she wrote it, that he would translate this into saying that the gentleman in question had a title.

But she thought it a mistake to put more than was absolutely necessary into the letter, just in case it gave him some hint in a strange way she had not foreseen that she was not husband hunting in London.

Packing her clothes was a long and tedious task. When they had finished she and Annie stood and surveyed the cases.

"Will we be able to take all these?" asked Annie.

"No, I don't think so. We'll have to leave a good deal behind and I can always buy more clothes when we arrive."

"Oh, miss," said Annie, suddenly struck by doubts. "Are you sure you're wise to travel alone with a man?"

"I won't be alone. I shall have you."

But she knew she was only avoiding the question. A maid did not count, because she was an employee and could be dismissed. Only a lady with authority was acceptable.

'And I have no chaperone,' she thought. 'So Pa must never know where I am.'

She therefore sat down and added a further page to her father's letter.

"*I have always thought,*" she wrote, "*that you and Mama were so very happy together. It is what I want myself and I therefore need a little more time to think over the position as it is at the moment.*

I love you, Papa, and I want you always to love me. I know that you are thinking of my happiness and you would be very upset if I was unhappy for the rest of my life.

I am merely going away to think things over and you are not to worry about me."

She finished her letter,

"Your affectionate and admiring daughter, Lexia."

She addressed the envelope to her father, hoping that he would not receive it until she and the Marquis were far away.

Just for a moment she felt afraid. Could she really be doing anything so outrageous socially, as well as being extremely disobedient to her father, as to run off with a strange man who she really knew very little about?

Then she told herself there was no need to be frightened as after all, the Marquis was a gentleman and, what mattered just as much, he was Frank, her true friend.

She was now so nervous that she was afraid her father would notice, so that afternoon she invented a headache as an excuse to stay in her room.

Fortunately he had invited some male friends over that evening for a card party, so she was not required to make an appearance.

By the time his friends had departed she had gone to bed, but she could not sleep. Thoughts of the step she was about to take crowded into her head and she became more apprehensive than she cared to admit, but she was determined not to give up now.

At last she climbed out of bed and went to the window to look up at the sky.

She had a feeling that her mother was in Heaven watching over her and she suddenly felt that she would understand as no one else would,

'You loved Papa and you were so happy together that is how I want to be, but men like Papa are few and far between. I can only pray, Mama darling, that I will find someone who will love me and I will love him and we will be as happy as you were.'

She felt the tears come into her eyes, but she brushed them away.

'I have to be strong and sensible over this,' she told herself. 'I am doing something which the world will think appalling, but I am going to do it, because I think it's the only way to live my own life in the way I want it. I will trust Frank and face whatever comes.'

She rose early and had breakfast with her father, fearful lest something should make him change his mind about the meet, but it seemed that he was set on going.

"I am very sorry, dearest, to be leaving you alone," he told her, "but I am anxious to play my part with the hounds. I am quite certain they will find me a great help."

Lexia knew they would welcome his money if nothing else, but she merely said,

"You are quite right, Papa. I am sure the hunt will need a great deal of help in the future."

If only, she thought, her father could be a little less naïve in his social climbing. She had a horrid suspicion that people laughed at him, even while they pocketed his cash, but she could not say this to him.

When it was time for him to depart, she went to the front door with her father and he kissed her goodbye.

"We must have a talk tomorrow," he said.

"About what, Pa?"

"Don't be demure with me, miss. You know very well about what. About how to bring his Lordship up to scratch.

I thought you had succeeded the other night but – well anyway, we'll talk. I'll probably be very late coming home tonight. It will turn into one of those affairs that – "

"A drinking party," smiled Lexia.

"What do you know about drinking parties, miss?" he demanded.

"Well, I have heard my father come home late a few times," she replied.

"That's enough. I never heard such – a well brought up young woman should not know such things."

Lexia gave him an eager hug.

"Goodbye, Pa dear! Enjoy yourself."

"I will. And don't call me Pa."

He walked out to his carriage and Lexia watched him go, feeling a lump in her throat. She loved him dearly even though she was defying him.

She wondered how long it would be before they met again and under what circumstances. Or perhaps he would refuse to meet her or even acknowledge her as his daughter.

For a moment her eyes blurred with tears, but she clung to her resolve. She could not afford to weaken now.

The biggest task was bringing the bags downstairs without being seen, but they managed by creeping down the back stairs very quietly, where they hid them in a room which was kept for extra rugs and cushions for the carriages.

Then she was on edge, terrified that something might happen to prevent her from being ready on time.

The day seemed to drag on and she watched the clock feeling that every moment seemed to take a hundred years.

At last, on the stroke of two o'clock, the butler informed her that there was a carriage for her at the back door.

He seemed rather surprised and Lexia said,

"Ah, yes, I am giving some clothes to be sold for the Cottage Hospital. I have put them in the little storage room, so perhaps someone can take them out for me."

A footman was sent to fetch the hidden luggage and loaded it in the carriage and at the last moment Lexia slipped into her father's study and placed the letter on his desk.

Then she hurried outside and when she saw the carriage she realised the Marquis had been very clever. It was not one of his recognisable vehicles with a coat of arms on the panel, but an ancient one, which had obviously not been painted for some time.

"Are you sure you would not like me to send one of our carriages to bring you back, miss?" asked the butler.

"No, thank you," replied Lexia hurriedly. "I am meeting some friends at the hospital and they have promised to bring me back."

The driver said nothing. He had obviously been told to keep his mouth shut.

She climbed in, followed by Annie and the driver started off.

Lexia sat in silence as they drove at a good pace, heading so she thought to the railway station, but instead to her surprise they drove through narrow lanes until they came to the river.

"But why are we here?" she asked in wonder.

Then she saw the Marquis walking up to the carriage to help her down.

Just behind him was Hawkins who began unloading her bags and taking them to the river.

"What are we doing?" she asked.

"I thought you would be surprised. Now hurry, I have arranged everything and we are going first by boat."

He led her to the river where there was a large rowing

boat powered by four oarsmen.

It was something Lexia had never done before and she felt it exciting to start the adventure with something new and original.

At the same time, she thought they could hardly be going to sea – in *this* boat? But there was no point in asking questions as she had committed herself to this adventure and vowed to cope with whatever happened.

So she took a seat in the back of the boat, while her luggage was piled up behind with what she thought must be the Marquis's.

Then the men's oars were dipped into the water and they started to move at what Lexia thought was a tremendous speed.

Only when the carriage in which they had travelled was almost out of sight did she say,

"Now it's happening, I can hardly believe we are here. It is nothing like anything I have ever done before."

"I don't want you to be disappointed," said the Marquis. "But be careful what you say in front of these oarsmen as they know us by our new names and they must not guess the truth."

He spoke almost in a whisper.

Lexia lapsed into silence, feeling almost as if she had walked into a dream and it could hardly be true.

They seemed to row for a long time, while the light faded and gradually the river broadened out.

"You will have realised that we are near the sea," the Marquis told her and there we will find the ship that will take us abroad."

"Where abroad?"

"To the Mediterranean. In a few hours we will be far out to sea and since we have already assumed our new names, we will appear to have vanished into thin air."

"What are our new names?"

"Edward Malcolm and his sister Agnes."

Lexia made a face.

"I don't think I like Agnes."

"I am afraid I had no choice. I had to obtain passports and I borrowed them from a friend, who owes me a favour. He has frequently travelled with his sister, so I was able to borrow both passports."

"To tell the truth, I was wondering what would happen about passports," she admitted. "I never thought of anything like this."

"We are desperate characters," he told her and Lexia laughed.

"I think you have been wonderfully clever."

Now the port was coming into view, crowded with boats.

"That's where we are headed," he said, pointing out a very large white steamer.

"It's huge," she exclaimed. "It's like the ship Pa and I were in when we sailed to England."

"It's the *Maybelle*," he said. "It's becoming quite well known for cruising the Mediterranean in great style. I cabled the Purser's Office for our accommodation and it was immediately confirmed, so we have only to go aboard."

Lexia drew in her breath. Her eyes were shining.

At last they reached the quay where Lexia found she was very stiff, but nothing mattered except the thrill of escape.

Together they boarded the *Maybelle* and at once Lexia could see that the Marquis had not been exaggerating. The *Maybelle* was indeed a luxury ship and everything about her confirmed it.

They went to the Purser's Office and just as the Marquis had promised, staterooms had been reserved for them.

"Our very best," the Purser confirmed. "As the most expensive they were the last to go and so they were still available when we received your cable, but I had another application only an hour later, so you were only just in time."

The Marquis paid and a Steward showed them below, where they found their luxurious staterooms side by side. They were both well furnished each with its own private bathroom.

When the Steward had departed Lexia went and knocked on the Marquis's door. When he had let her in, she said,

"How brilliant of you. How ever did you find this magnificent ship?"

"I thought we had a better chance of seeing Europe this way than any other. I have been on a journey on one of these ships before, where I found the food was excellent and the service good and as we are exploring the world for ourselves, we might as well be comfortable about it."

"I still think I am dreaming," sighed Lexia. "Have we really managed to escape?"

"I certainly hope so. I expect your father is still at the meet, which will go on for hours and the servants who gossip in my house will have no idea where I really am. At least, I sincerely hope not."

"And now our great adventure starts."

The Marquis nodded.

"This is the kind of adventure I used to dream about when I was eighteen," he said. "Now, at last, my dream has come true."

"Nonsense! exclaimed Lexia. "You must have had

lots of exciting things happen to you – far more than me – a man always does. Oh, if only we can be successful! It would be too terrible to come back empty-handed."

"We will have only ourselves to blame if we do. By the way, I think we should keep out of sight until we are out to sea, which I gather will be in about half-an-hour."

He walked to the porthole.

"I can see people coming on board now. Cross your fingers that they won't guess who we really are."

"If they are holidaymakers they won't be concerned with anyone but themselves," observed Lexia.

"That's true enough. Who will worry about two unimportant people, who have nothing to recommend them but their appearance?"

Lexia laughed.

"I thought you were going to say their pockets. You booked us the most expensive accommodation."

"I could hardly expect you to travel any other way, especially if you want to meet congenial company, perhaps even a future husband."

"I suppose I shouldn't ask too much, but you never know! Perhaps the Gods will be on our side and we will find exactly what we are seeking."

"At the very least," he said, "just being with people who have no idea who we are will be a change and if we want to be convincing, we too should forget our true identities. If our enterprise succeeds we may live happily ever after. But if we fail – you know what will happen."

Lexia nodded.

"Marriage," she murmured darkly. "*To each other*."

They both shuddered.

CHAPTER SEVEN

When Lexia and Annie had put all her clothes away it was time to dress for dinner.

She was in a mood to celebrate, so she chose a gown of pale green silk, with matching lace flounces. Around her neck she wore a three-stranded gold chain. She knew that she looked her best and she saw it in the Marquis's eyes when he came to collect her.

He himself was fine in evening clothes and she wondered why he had not been able to find a woman to love him for himself. Surely a man so handsome must draw all eyes.

They walked to the upper deck where the dining room was situated and he escorted her to her chair. They were seated by a window, through which she could see that the coast was already out of sight and the sun was setting on the water.

"Now that we have a moment to breathe," began Lexia excitedly, "I want to know everything. So far, all you've told me is that we are going to the Mediterranean."

"We'll be crossing the Bay of Biscay tonight," he replied, "then going South to our first stop in Gibraltar and after that we'll hug the coast of Spain for a while and stop in Valencia. From there we will go straight on to Greece."

"Greece?" she echoed. "How wonderful. I have

always wanted to see that country. Will we be there long?"

"We have one day in Athens and two days touring the Greek islands."

Lexia gave a cry.

"The islands! They have always sounded so romantic and exciting."

"And of course, one of them belongs to Apollo, the God of Love."

"It gets more thrilling every moment," cried Lexia. "I had no idea, when we escaped, that you would be so clever as to find a ship which was going to all the places I have always wanted to visit."

"It was just a bit of luck," confessed the Marquis, "but I do agree with you that we have been very fortunate."

"What happens after that?"

"After Greece we begin the journey back and we will stop in different ports than we did on the way out – Sicily, Naples, Monte Carlo."

"The perfect trip," she sighed blissfully.

"I hope so. Now, let's have something to eat."

As they studied the menu she murmured,

"Did you manage to settle things with your creditors?"

"I sent most of the money to London to be put into the hands of the man who handles my affairs and he will see to everything. The rest of the money I used to book our tickets on this ship."

"So I sent you enough?"

"It was far more than I expected," he said uneasily. "In fact I had a big shock when I saw the amount."

Lexia had a feeling of walking on thin ice. Any mention of her vast wealth was awkward for him and she was not quite sure how to make it less so.

Somehow the lessons in etiquette she had received never seemed to cover this kind of situation.

"Frank, please don't feel badly about the money. You will be spending most of it on me."

"I am glad to hear it."

"As you did when you bought our travel tickets," she hurried on, "and you will be paying all our expenses, which is why – "

She took a deep breath.

"I have brought some more money with me and I want you to take it, because I wouldn't feel safe carrying it about myself."

To her relief he laughed.

"Lexia, the diplomatic service lost a genius in you!"

His eyes told her that he had understood her desperate attempts at tact and appreciated them.

"I promise you," he declared stoutly, "that somehow, some day, I will pay you back."

"I don't want you to," said Lexia at once. "It is I who am in your debt for coming with me. I could never have made this trip alone and you have made it possible and the money is my contribution."

She then rather spoiled her effect by adding comically,

"Besides we are in this mess together and if we can get out of it without disaster, then what does it matter who pays the bills?"

The Marquis laughed.

"Thank you a million times. It is no use pretending that I am not grateful, because I am."

"Well I did rather blackmail you into coming with me, didn't I?"

"Yes," he agreed promptly and they both chuckled.

95

A waiter hovered beside them.

"Mr. Malcolm?"

When the Marquis did not react, Lexia said hastily,

"Yes, this is Mr. Malcolm."

"Are you ready to give me your order now, sir?"

"Yes," he said hurriedly, frowning at Lexia to stop her laughing.

When the waiter had gone she giggled,

"Who was it told me not to forget my new identity?"

He grinned sheepishly.

"You'd think I would have remembered, wouldn't you? I am so glad to get rid of the title for a while.

"You see, I have always been bullied about my position and the first thing I remember was being told I was too important to do this and that. When I grew older they told me that, as I was so important, I must do this and I must do that and all the things I really didn't want to do. But now just for a short time, let me forget it!"

He paused thoughtfully, before he added,

"In fact I intend to enjoy this trip as I have never enjoyed anything before and I want you to do the same."

"And I am going to have the time of my life," said Lexia, her eyes sparkling.

He regarded her tenderly.

"You look so pretty when you make a remark like that," he told her, "that I am sure any man would be at your feet in no time."

"I do hope so and I want you to be lucky too. You must have a look at the girls on board and be very careful to fall in love with the right one and not be swept off your feet by the first beauty who smiles at you."

"I promise not to be, ma'am."

"You must have had plenty of experience of beauties smiling at you," she observed cheekily. "Well, I know you have, because I saw for myself at Lady Overton's."

"But the beauties will think I am just plain Mr. Malcolm," he reminded her. "So perhaps they won't bother to smile."

There was no danger of that, she thought. He was easily the most attractive man in the restaurant.

Then a startling idea came to her. She gasped and put her hands to her cheeks.

"Lexia, what is it?" he asked at once.

"Oh, Frank, I've just had the most terrible thought."

"For goodness sake, tell me."

"I can't bear to. It's so awful – "

He went pale.

"I beg you not to keep me in suspense. Tell me at once if some new danger has occurred to you."

"The worst danger of all," she moaned.

"*Tell me!*"

"We are embarking on this trip," she said solemnly, "in an attempt to find love as ourselves, not a man with a title and a woman with money, but just as people. In doing so, we shall discover our true worth in the eyes of others."

She took a deep breath.

"Frank, have you thought of what we might discover?"

She dropped her voice melodramatically.

"*Suppose we have no worth!*"

For a moment he stared at her and then he sat back in his chair, blowing out his cheeks and covering his eyes with his hands.

"Lexia, don't scare me like that."

She grinned impishly at him.

"You are a terrible, terrible girl," he scolded, trying to sound severe through his laughter.

"I know I am. I just can't help it. And actually, it's something we ought to consider. We just blithely assumed everyone would want us anyway. Suppose they don't?"

He nodded.

"We might find out that we are nothing without our worldly advantages. What a shocking prospect! Let's immediately drink champagne and banish the thought."

He began to laugh again and she joined in.

Suddenly she knew a moment of pure happiness, such as she had never known before. To be sitting here and laughing with him was the nicest thing she had ever done.

"We're both crazy," he exclaimed.

"Yes," she agreed happily. "Yes, we are."

He filled both their glasses with champagne and raised his. She raised hers and they clinked.

"To us," he toasted. "To our escape and above all, to the future."

*

It was night when they passed through the Bay of Biscay and the passage was less rough than Lexia had feared.

In fact after the first hour when Lexia stayed awake because she was a little nervous, she fell into a pleasant dreamless sleep.

She awoke just as the ship was gliding into Gibraltar.

'So far, so good,' she told herself. 'We have escaped and everything has gone so well so far.'

She had breakfast in her cabin, thinking it wiser not to go exploring without Frank, as she now thought of him. In fact she was dressed and growing a little impatient when he arrived.

"Good morning!" he called. "As I expect you've seen through the porthole, it's a lovely morning with lots of sunshine."

"Are we going ashore?" she asked eagerly.

"No, I think we must give up that pleasure. There are too many English ships here and too much chance of us being recognised."

"*You* being recognised," she asserted. "Your face must be better known than mine. Are you sure no one has seen you?"

"Quite sure. But since we dare not go ashore, why don't we spend the day exploring the ship? It's so big that it will be almost as good as exploring a City."

Lexia found that he was right. The *Maybelle* was built to carry over a thousand passengers and five hundred crew and was equipped with five restaurants, a variety of shops and a theatre.

There was even a shop selling English newspapers, which they picked up in various ports.

"But the ones they will buy in Gibraltar will be two days old," he explained. "So, even if our flight has been discovered, we won't be in the newspapers yet."

Lexia shuddered.

"Don't. I don't even want to think about it."

A memory came back to her.

"Now that you are here let me give you the money to look after, as we agreed last night."

But when she took it out things began to go wrong.

"Two thousand pounds!" he exclaimed horrified. "I had no idea you were talking about so much."

"It's the same as before – "

"That was different. That was to set this trip up and pay necessary expenses, but – this – I am sorry Lexia, I cannot explain – I cannot take this kind of money from you."

There was a look of revulsion on his face that alarmed her. Money meant so little to her that she had not quite appreciated just how the lack of it felt to him, but she sensed that if she put another foot wrong there would be a disaster.

"You are right," she agreed. "I will keep it. This drawer locks and it will be quite safe."

She locked the money back in the drawer and turned to him smiling. He smiled back, although it looked a little forced, as she guessed did her own.

They both had the feeling of having come to the edge of a cliff and only just escaped.

"Let's go and take a walk," he proposed.

For the next hour they enjoyed a stroll in the sunshine from one end of the ship to another.

"I think it would be a good idea to look in at the Purser's Office," suggested the Marquis. "I have had an idea that might help us."

Once in the office he enquired casually,

"I suppose there is no chance of my having a look at the passenger list, just in case I spot any of my friends?"

"I am not really supposed to do that," the Purser began to say.

A note changed hands – the list appeared and the Purser left the room.

The Marquis quickly ran his eyes down the two hundred and fifty First Class passengers and heaved a sigh of relief.

"No names that I recognise, but I suppose I should check the rest."

Two hundred Second Class and six hundred Third class passengers failed to produce any cause for concern.

Relieved, they were about to depart when the Purser

returned.

"Thank you," said the Marquis. "I found nobody."

"What a shame! Lord and Lady Allerton were supposed to come on this sailing, but at the last moment they changed their minds."

"Indeed?" replied the Marquis, glassy-eyed. "How interesting! Good day to you!"

Seizing Lexia's arm he ushered her firmly out of the office.

"Frank, what is it?"

"We've just escaped disaster by the skin of our teeth. Allerton is one of my oldest friends."

As if by a signal they grasped each other's hands and began to run and did not stop until they reached the deck.

"Why are we running?" Frank asked her as they reached the rail. "It can make no difference now."

"I just feel safer up here in the open air," Lexia told him. "What a narrow escape!"

"Well, it proves that Providence is on our side. Now let us cast care aside and promenade on the deck until we have calmed down."

They made a handsome couple strolling in the sun and many admiring glances were cast at them, both from men and women.

"I must say, I am not impressed by anyone I can see," the Marquis remarked. "I don't think I could approve of you associating with any of them."

"*You* couldn't approve – ?"

"Do not forget that you are my sister and I have to look after you and protect you from the men who would pursue you."

Lexia laughed.

"You take your duties very seriously, Frank, but please remember that *I* have to look after *you* in the same way."

The Marquis chuckled.

"You protect me and I will protect you. This is the start of chapter one in the most exciting drama there has ever been."

"You must tell me when you reach the last chapter, if the book will be a success or a failure," she asked him.

"It will be the success we make it, which means that our success is assured."

"I only hope you are right," replied Lexia.

"You will learn I am always right and I intend to continue being so."

*

As twilight fell the ship pulled out of Gibraltar and began the trip to Valencia. Lexia was looking forward to seeing that City, but first she had something else in mind.

"The ship has a casino," she told Frank. "Let's have dinner early and then go and play."

"Gambling? I am not sure that I approve."

"Nonsense! In my brother's company I shall be perfectly respectable."

"Just the same – " he teased.

"I shall stamp on your foot any minute!" she threatened.

"In that case, I give in."

The casino was a blaze of light and colour as Lexia entered on the Marquis's arm with a skip in her step and looked around her thrilled.

She had dressed a little more daringly tonight in an off-the-shoulder gown of deep blue. Sapphires adorned her throat and ears.

Her hair had been dressed more extravagantly than usual with three perky little blue feathers springing from her elaborate coiffure. It had taken her a while to get those feathers right and Annie had had to change them several times.

"I want to look *adventurous*," she had said with relish.

And it had taken her three feathers to look as adventurous as she wanted and she would have preferred four, but Annie flatly refused, saying four would make her look like a hussy.

But three were doing their work very nicely she thought as the Marquis was looking at her worriedly, not quite knowing what to make of her. That was all right. She didn't mind confusing him a little, but there was admiration in his eyes too.

"You look beautiful," he sighed.

"You don't think I am scandalous for wanting to be here?"

"There are plenty of other ladies present."

But there were none, he realised, who looked so much at home. As she strolled on his arm from table to table, he could see that she understood everything that she saw.

"Tell me," he murmured, "exactly what did you learn in the California gold fields."

She smiled, understanding him perfectly.

"I learned to play poker."

"*You are not playing poker here!*"

"Don't worry. I'll restrain myself."

"So I should hope," he said fervently.

She paused by the roulette table and watched with interest as gamblers laid their bets and the wheel spun.

"Lexia, why don't we – ?"

"No, I want to place a bet. I am feeling lucky tonight."

Somebody was just rising from the table and quick as a flash Lexia slid into the vacant seat, but as there was only one, the Marquis had to content himself with standing behind her and trying to restrain her from that position.

In this he was entirely unsuccessful, but he doubted if he would have been any luckier sitting beside her. Lexia bore all the marks of someone who had the bit between her teeth.

Her first bet was lucky and she won a small amount. The second gave her a big win.

"You see?" she boasted, looking up at the Marquis. "I told you I was lucky. Why don't you play too?"

"No, thank you. One of us needs to keep a little common sense."

"Good. That can be you."

The man sitting beside her laughed at this sally.

"Well done, ma'am. I like a lady of spirit."

The Marquis regarded him with disfavour, disliking his heavy build, black moustache and thick lips. Lexia, he was annoyed to see, appeared charmed by him, actually laughing at the remark as though it had been witty.

"Would you honour me, ma'am, by placing a bet for me?" he asked.

"Black twenty-five," she said at once.

The man immediately put his chips on black twenty-five. Lexia chose red twenty-two.

The wheel spun.

Black twenty-five.

The man cheered and Lexia gave a little squeal of delight. It had an inane sound, quite unlike her normal self, the Marquis might have thought, if his mind had not been in turmoil.

"I think we should leave," he urged Lexia.

"No, you mustn't go now," the man boomed, seizing Lexia's hand. "You're my lucky mascot. I need you."

He scooped up his winnings, shoving a small portion of them towards Lexia.

"You see, I did win?" she squealed at the Marquis.

"You won less than your stake," he pointed out.

"What does that matter? I won."

"Of course it matters," he tried to point out. "You are losing money."

"Oh, never mind! I am enjoying myself."

He nearly tore his hair.

"Lexia, if you thought black twenty-five was the right choice, why didn't you bet on it too?"

"Where's the fun in that?" she asked with a shrug.

"*Place your bets, please.*"

"Red eighteen," Lexia said at once.

The man pushed his chips onto red eighteen and she did the same.

The wheel spun.

Red eighteen.

Lexia and her companion gave a shout of joy and then he seized her hand, covering it with kisses, which cast Lexia into giggles.

"My name is Alaric Carnoustie," he declared passionately.

With difficulty the Marquis repressed a snort, whilst Lexia beamed at the man still holding her hand.

"Mine is Le- "

"Agnes!" called the Marquis warningly.

"Agnes Malcolm," she corrected herself quickly.

"And this is my brother, Edward."

"Ah, a brother!" purred Alaric. "For a moment I feared he was your husband."

"Oh, no, he is not my husband. How could you have thought that? Look, I'm not wearing a wedding ring?"

"True, but if not a husband, he might have been – " Alaric leaned forward and mumbled in her ear.

Lexia gave a shriek of laughter.

"Oh, what a shocking thing to say!" she cried, giving Alaric a reproving tap with her fan. "He isn't that, either."

"May I share the joke?" enquired the Marquis in a dangerously pleasant voice.

"Oh, I don't think so," came back Lexia. "I doubt if you would appreciate it."

"On the contrary, I feel fairly sure I could assess it at its true value," he replied icily.

"Well, we don't want that, do we?" tittered Lexia.

"*Place your bets, please.*"

This time Alaric Carnoustie's lucky mascot failed him and they both lost. Lexia promptly bet again and then again.

The Marquis tried once more to persuade her to leave, but she shrugged him aside again.

He began to feel as if he was living in a nightmare and to add to his troubles, the bosom of Lexia's gown was revealing. It was not lower than was normal in an evening gown, but the Marquis, standing above and behind her, had to keep reminding himself that he was a gentleman.

What could not be denied was that her shape was ravishingly attractive and he had never been so conscious of her before.

Alaric Carnoustie seemed as indifferent to his losses as Lexia was to hers. He insisted that she was bringing him luck in the face of compelling evidence to the contrary.

When he begged for *just a little keepsake*, Lexia whisked one of her blue feathers out of her hair and presented it to him, which sent him into transports of delight.

Worse, he seemed to have taken possession of her hand and either sat clutching it or covered it with kisses in a way that made the Marquis want to knock him to the floor.

Lexia was clearly having a wonderful time, despite the fact that she lost repeatedly and his alarm grew.

"We should leave *now*," he insisted, laying a hand on her arm.

"Go away and stop being such a spoil sport," she pouted.

"You are losing too much."

She shrugged.

"Lex- *Agnes*!"

"Why don't you leave her alone?" Carnoustie demanded in a voice that was not entirely sober.

"I advise you to be silent, sir," the Marquis told him in a freezing voice.

"And I advise you to mind your own business! You are only her brother. It's not as though – "

But suddenly Carnoustie fell silent. He could not have said why, except that something in Mr. Malcolm's eyes made the words die in his throat.

The Marquis's hand on Lexia's arm tightened.

"We are leaving now," he ordered softly. "You can either come willingly or I can throw you over my shoulder and carry you out. It's up to you."

Looking into his eyes, Lexia read real intent.

"I must go," she said sweetly to Carnoustie. "It's been delightful knowing you."

He kissed her hand.

"Perhaps we'll meet again," he sighed.

"No," the Marquis intervened shortly. "You won't."

Keeping Lexia's hand firmly in his he made his way out of the casino.

"Hey!" she said.

"Have you taken leave of your senses?" he demanded furiously. "Whatever possessed you?"

"I was enjoying – myself," she stammered, speaking breathlessly, for he was moving at a fast pace.

"You have no right to enjoy yourself like that."

They had reached her stateroom and he waited while she took out her key and then came in behind her and closed the door.

"Do you know how much you lost tonight?"

"Actually I stopped counting."

"Stopped – ? Give me patience! Of all the irresponsible – you shouldn't be allowed out with money if you don't know how to handle it."

"But that's what I told *you*," she cried, "and I asked you to take care of it for me and you wouldn't, so what could I do when you were so unkind – ?"

"All right, all right," he said hastily. "Give it to me now."

She opened her bag for him to take out the notes inside and then unlocked the drawer where the rest was kept and handed the bundle to him.

He eyed her suspiciously.

"If I thought you had done this on purpose – "

"*Me*?"

"Don't give me that innocent look," he growled. "I am beginning to know you and you are capable of any trick.

Lexia!"

There was something about the way she was looking at him that frayed his control and he put his hands on her shoulders, looking hard into her face.

"Lexia," he repeated, "you must try to be sensible."

For some reason she was breathing hard, her beautiful bosom rising and falling.

"If either of us was sensible," she sighed dreamily, "we wouldn't be here."

He gave her a little shake.

"Stop trying to trip me up, you wretched girl. You nearly turned me white-haired with your antics tonight and as for the way you behaved with Carnoustie – "

"Careful, *Edward*!" she said with a hint of danger in her voice. "If I want to flirt a little, it really doesn't concern my brother."

"It most certainly does!" he screamed, suddenly filled with a kind of rage. "And you were not 'doing a little flirting', you were making an exhibition of yourself."

"How dare you! I did no such thing!"

"You practically made him a present of your hand and I am surprised it's still attached to you."

Lexia's eyes glinted with real anger.

"Now you're just being insulting," she bellowed, trying to pull away.

For an answer, his hands tightened on her shoulders, drawing her closer. He knew he was being unwise and that he should stop now and walk out, but somehow he couldn't.

The Marquis had never noticed how large and lovely her eyes were, but now that they were so close to him he could not avoid their impact.

"Lexia – " he started uncertainly. "I want to – "

"What?" she whispered.

But no more words would come. His heart was thundering and the world seemed to be turning about him and suddenly he was unsure of everything that had been so clear earlier.

Gradually he began lowering his head.

She did not reach up to him, but neither did she pull away. She seemed transfixed, her eyes gazing into his as though she was waiting – hoping – for something.

In another moment his lips would touch hers.

And then reality burst in, shattering the pleasant dream that had been slowly enveloping him.

This was a betrayal.

He had promised to care for her and not take advantage of her. Now he was betraying that trust.

He stepped back sharply, releasing her so suddenly that she had to grasp at something to steady herself. She did not know what it was, she was in a daze.

"As long as we've got that clear," he said. "I'll take care of the money – the money, where is it?"

"On the floor. You dropped it when – when – "

"Yes, I did, didn't I?"

He hastily seized the notes up from the floor and left without saying goodnight.

He had one further matter to attend to before he could consider the matter closed.

Late that night he knocked on Alaric Carnoustie's door.

When the door was opened, he entered without waiting for an invitation. A short scuffle ensued, after which he departed, somewhat dishevelled and clutching a blue feather.

CHAPTER EIGHT

At Valencia they hired a carriage and spent a day sightseeing. Lexia returned to the ship weighed down with souvenirs which, as the Marquis pointed out to her, were useless and worthless.

"You sound like Pa," she told him. "He never lets me buy trinkets because he says they have no value and he likes to receive 'value for every penny'."

"What about sentimental value?"

"He doesn't know what the words mean, but one day I shall be glad of my souvenirs. When I am old, I shall look at this – " she showed him a large, red paper flower, "and remember that you bought it for me on the most wonderful trip of my life."

He grinned sheepishly.

They were strolling along the deck, waiting for the ship to cast off.

"Have you seen any of the new passengers who came aboard?" he asked.

"Yes, there's a crowd who seem to be Spanish from the way they were talking. Look, there they are at the far end of the deck."

A group of four people were strolling towards them. In the centre was a tall statuesque woman with a well developed figure and an air of magnificence. Her clothing was costly in an exaggerated style and jewels dripped from her. She walked like a queen who expected tribute from all about her.

With her were two men and another woman, who gave the impression of being satellites hovering around a planet.

A few more steps brought her within sight of the Marquis and Lexia.

She stopped and looked them up and down.

Then she seemed to dismiss Lexia and fix her attention on the Marquis. Her eyes flickered over him taking in every detail.

She smiled and it was a luscious smile that curved her full lips extravagantly, as everything about her was extravagant. The smile was heavy with meaning.

At last she passed on, her retinue trailing meekly behind her and the Marquis and Lexia breathed out.

"My goodness!" she exclaimed.

"That was as good as a circus," he said.

"Frank!" She thumped his arm gently. "That was a dreadful thing to say. She's probably a great lady."

"I am sure she is, but she terrifies me. Did you see how she looked at me – as though I was something she was planning to eat for breakfast?"

Lexia had observed the look, but it seemed to her that the Marquis had definitely misread it and that the Spanish lady had other plans in mind. She had noticed too the way she had looked at her or rather had refused to look at her, thus clearly considering her as of no account.

And that was a challenge that could not be ignored.

There was another passenger, a young man, who caught her attention. He was extremely handsome in a rather coarse way, but despite his looks she could not warm to him.

He too noticed her, fixing his eyes on her in a way she

found displeasing. He was practically leering and it did not seem to occur to him that she might object to his behaviour.

She noticed him again when she and the Marquis had taken their seats in the dining room. He had reserved the best table and the waiters served him with an air of obsequiousness.

"Who is that man?" Lexia asked their waiter.

"That is Mr. Storton, ma'am. His father owns the shipyard that made this vessel."

"Really?" said Lexia, trying to sound indifferent, which was hard because the Marquis had just nudged her ankle under the table.

"What did you mean by that?" she asked him when the waiter had gone.

"Maybe he is the one you are seeking."

"Goodness, I hope not!"

"He might be your destiny, the one for whom you have travelled the oceans – "

"If you don't stop talking like that, I really shall kick you," she replied crossly. "He is a disgusting slug and sooner than marry him I'd – I'd – I'd – even marry *you*!"

The Marquis grinned.

"And you can't say worse about any one man than that, can you?"

"*No!*"

"I don't know what you find the matter with him, as he obviously admires you from the way he's staring at you and he must be rich in his own right, so he isn't after your money."

Before she could answer the young man rose and approached them.

"Allow me to introduce myself," he began. "Samuel Storton. Miss Malcolm, Mr. Malcolm."

"You know who we are?" she asked.

"It was easy to find out. My father owns this ship, in fact, he built her."

So he had checked the passenger list, but far from being flattered, Lexia was annoyed by this revelation and she felt as though he had spied on her.

He sat down without waiting to be asked and proceeded to deliver a monologue about himself.

"I have to travel on his vessels from time to time to see if they are working properly," he explained. "The Pater couldn't do without my reports."

Lexia listened, nodding, saying yes and no and privately suspecting that 'the Pater' had adopted this method as a way of keeping a useless son out of the house for weeks at a time.

There seemed no way to get rid of him.

When their meal was over they all moved to the ballroom.

"I am longing to dance with you," he declared.

Lexia had no desire to dance with him, but it was better than sitting listening to him.

As they circled the floor she noticed the Spaniards they had seen that afternoon. They were clearly wealthy people with a certain haughtiness that was imposing.

They had divided into couples, dancing together. The woman at the centre was tall and magnificent with flashing dark eyes and she danced as though she knew that she commanded everyone's attention.

As the dance ended she pulled away from her partner and marched boldly up to the table where the Marquis was sitting.

"We dance well together," asserted Samuel Storton. "We must dance again."

"No, thank you," Lexia declined him firmly, detaching herself and joining the Marquis, arriving in time to hear the Spanish woman say,

"They tell me you are English."

He rose, bowing gracefully to her.

"Edward Malcolm, at your service, ma'am, and this is my sister, Agnes."

The beauty flicked a glance at 'Agnes', barely greeted her and returned her attention to 'Edward'.

"I am the Señora Juanita Engracia Sofia Raiña Cadiz and I have found that Englishmen dance as well, if not better, than the Spanish," she crooned in a deep heavily accented voice. "Will you prove to me that this is true?"

"Well, I – "

The Señora tossed her head imperiously.

"Englishmen are shy about taking to the floor, while the Spanish spring onto it the moment the music starts."

The Marquis smiled.

"I will be delighted to dance with you."

"My cousin Dionisio will look after your sister. He fancies he is as good as the English when it comes to moving on the dance floor and I know he would love to dance with her."

She made an imperious gesture and he came forward. He was tall and pleasant looking, but there was nothing distinguished about him.

He bowed politely to Lexia, expressed himself honoured and gave her his hand. He seemed to find nothing strange in being virtually commanded to dance with her to suit the Señora's convenience.

Nor, she noticed, did the Marquis seem to mind being summoned to dance with this arrogant lady.

Mr. Storton melted away to her infinite relief.

Lexia took the floor with Dionisio and had to admit that he moved well. She began to enjoy herself, despite the behaviour of the Señora, who was dancing very closely in a rather exaggerated manner with the Marquis.

Despite what he had said earlier about being terrified of her, he seemed to be enjoying her company.

"Are you travelling very far?" Dionisio asked Lexia politely.

"Oh, just around the Mediterranean. And you?"

"I don't know. It's up to Juanita and since she became a widow she is a law unto herself."

"A widow?" echoed Lexia. "Did her husband die long ago?"

"Six months, but it was not a happy marriage. He was a tyrant and her parents had forced her to marry him because he was so rich. However, he died and left her all his money, so everything was for the best."

"I – really?"

She could think of nothing else to say in response to this kind of realism.

Clearly Juanita was not grieving.

"Who are the two people with you?" she asked him politely.

"They are Juanita's sister and her husband on their honeymoon. It pleases her to have them with us."

And clearly whatever pleased Juanita was law.

"She does indeed seem to be enjoying herself," observed Lexia.

"Oh, yes," Dionisio said at once. "She says after all she suffered in her marriage she is going to enjoy herself very much now and then she will find another husband, but he must be very, very different from the first."

"Really!"

"And she says that with him she will share a great passion."

"So she's looking for another Spaniard. I hear they're known as a very passionate race."

This was a mistake as Dionisio immediately held her closer, looking down at her with a sensual droop to his mouth that would have made her want to laugh if she had not been so agitated.

"We are certainly a passionate race," he declared huskily. "It pleases me that you understand."

"Not me," she replied, exasperated beyond endurance. "I am talking about your cousin."

"She does not think Spaniards are passionate. She is bored with them and says that Englishmen are *much* more interesting."

"Englishmen are *not* passionate," asserted Lexia firmly. "She is wrong about that."

"She says not and although they appear cool and controlled, that is only on the surface. She says that underneath an Englishman is a volcano waiting for the right woman to inspire him to glory!"

"Nonsense!" exclaimed Lexia. "That is a myth."

"Juanita does not think so. She says when an Englishman is inspired – "

"Yes, I understand," Lexia interrupted him hastily.

"I think my cousin and your brother enjoy each other's company very much," murmured Dionisio, glancing across the floor to where the other couple were swaying.

Unwillingly Lexia followed his gaze. The Marquis seemed to be moving in a trance, looking down at the Señora with brooding eyes, as though determined to take in every detail of her.

And that included her extremely low-cut gown, Lexia

decided, thoroughly annoyed by now.

It was positively disgraceful, the way that woman seemed to be showing everything.

Her shoulders were warm and creamy, the perfect background for the rubies around her neck and an exotic scent arose from her. Lexia had received a hint of it when they met and knew that it was hot and musky. She could only imagine what it was doing to the Marquis at close range.

"Does it not seem to you that they are growing very close?" asked Dionisio.

"Exceedingly," snapped Lexia.

"Soon she will inspire him to glory."

Lexia set her jaw and refused to answer him.

"He is fighting her," whispered Dionisio, "but he cannot resist. At any moment the volcano – "

"I am a little tired," came in Lexia hastily. "I would like to sit down."

He escorted her back to her table and attempted to make conversation until at last, defeated by her listless air, he took himself off.

Now she was alone and surely Frank would return soon? She looked around the floor, trying to find him and perhaps catch his attention.

But he was nowhere to be seen, nor was the Señora.

They had vanished together.

She looked again, trying to believe that she was mistaken, but there was still no sign of either of them.

What she did see, advancing on her like doom, was the awful Samuel Storton.

'I think it's time I retired to bed,' she told herself hastily.

She felt very lonely as she slipped out of the ballroom without anyone seeming to take any notice of her.

She knew that she should not blame the Marquis as something like this was bound to happen sooner or later.

'But he's become like my big brother. That's what he is – my brother and you don't expect your brother to desert you.'

As she approached her stateroom she could not help slowing, just to hear if any noise was coming from the Marquis's room next door. It was not the same as eaves-dropping, she told herself. She was merely concerned for him.

But there was total silence from the other side of the door and relieved, she went on her way.

With Annie's help, she undressed herself and climbed into bed.

'Perhaps I shouldn't have left without telling Frank,' she thought, 'but how could I tell him, when I didn't know where he was? Besides he might have thought I was expecting him to leave too.'

After all, she thought glumly, they had come on this strange adventure to meet other people rather than those who were chosen for them.

'I'd have enjoyed myself more if Dionisio had not been such a bore. He danced well, but his cousin seems to be his only topic of conversation and he certainly was not as interested in me as she is in Frank.'

She turned over in bed and tried to go to sleep, but she could not help listening to hear if Frank's door opened.

But there was no sound and she thought by this time Juanita would have taken him out on deck and would be flirting with him in the moonlight.

'Oh, nonsense! She isn't at all the kind of woman he

119

admires.'

She said it to herself again and then she said it again, but the truth was that she did not know the kind of woman he admired.

Juanita was beautiful and rich and he had found her for himself.

That might be all he needed and then it struck her that perhaps if Frank was really intrigued by the Señora, she might find herself very neglected and lonely.

'Oh, please God,' she prayed, 'don't let this adventure end too quickly.'

It was a cry which came from her heart.

She knew she should be sensible and the Marquis was only doing what they had planned, but she could not help being disappointed.

Something had gone wrong and she could not quite work out what it was.

As she fell asleep she was still trying to hear any sound from next door and pretending to herself that she was not doing so.

*

The next morning, when she woke, she found the sun pouring through her porthole and she knew there was another glorious day ahead.

But then she remembered the events of the night before and the sun seemed to go in.

She had not heard the Marquis return last night, so he must have stayed up late with his wealthy Spanish widow. Perhaps they had gone on dancing.

Or they had strolled the deck in the moonlight.

Or perhaps she had lured him into her cabin.

'She is very attractive,' thought Lexia, 'and he would

have found it difficult not to respond to her when she was determined to attract him, but it's too quick. I am not ready. I wanted Frank to myself for just a little longer.'

Or perhaps a lot longer.

She tried to laugh, but it did not sound very convincing to her own ears.

She had breakfast in bed, but she did not eat very much. Her appetite had suddenly deserted her.

She was just thinking that she should get up and dress, when there was a knock on the door.

Annie opened it and Lexia heard the Marquis say,

"May I come in?"

"One moment," she called, reaching for her bed jacket.

She could not allow him to see her in a low cut silk nightgown, but the bed jacket would make it proper.

"Come in," she called.

Annie stepped aside to let him pass and he entered her room smiling.

"I had breakfast in bed," she explained, "as I had no idea what time you went to bed. You might have wanted to sleep until luncheon time."

He came towards her bed and, sat down on it, saying,

"You slipped away so quickly last night that for a moment I was frightened you had fallen overboard."

Lexia laughed.

"You were never frightened of anything so stupid. I could see there was no chance of my getting a word in edgeways, so after dancing twice with Dionisio, which was quite enough, I went to bed."

"That was very sensible of you and you missed very little."

Lexia looked at him.

"Are you telling me that *you* missed anything," she enquired archly, "because I find it hard to believe you."

"She was very persistent, but somehow I managed to get away. I listened at your door when I came to bed, but everything was quiet and I didn't want to wake you up."

"Did you enjoy yourself?"

"I would have enjoyed it a great deal more if I had not felt it a mistake to become involved too soon," he answered.

"In other words you ran away," she teased.

"I suppose I did, but some instinct warned me that the lady was trouble and, having just escaped one difficulty, it seemed to me unwise to walk straight into another."

He saw her regarding him quizzically.

"So, if you want the truth," he said, "I came to bed alone and, strange though it may seem, I slept peacefully."

"So it all ended well this time," she laughed. "On the other hand, perhaps you should consider her seriously as she is very rich or didn't you know about that?"

"Oh, yes I did," he muttered gloomily. "She told me all about it. Then she told me again and then again. Thank goodness they are leaving the ship today."

"Well, that is a relief at any rate," agreed Lexia.

"A relief?"

"Well – " suddenly flustered at what she had betrayed, she stammered, "It would be nice if it happened to us both at the same time, so that one of us isn't just left – I mean, you did seem very taken with her and – "

"Lexia," he said softly, "I am not as foolish as you think I am."

The way he spoke was so heavy with meaning that for a moment she could not think what to say.

"That is very unfair," she protested at last. "I don't think you are a fool. I think you are very clever. I am only frightened that you will be swept away by some woman who is not worthy of you."

"Let me tell you one thing. If I have learned nothing else, I have learned to be suspicious. If you reach for the stars, you must tell yourself that only the stars will do and never settle for less!"

"And Juanita isn't the stars?"

"No, Juanita is more of a planet. Probably Mars, the harbinger of war."

"That sounds very interesting," said Lexia demurely, her imp of jealousy not quite dead.

He grinned.

"Let's just say that she is not part of my plans, nor likely to be."

She poured herself another cup of tea and then the Marquis said unexpectedly,

"You look very lovely in bed."

"What did you say?" queried Lexia, hardly able to believe her ears.

"I have always thought that women look particularly attractive when they lie back against a lace-trimmed pillow and their hair touches their shoulders."

Lexia stared at him.

She had a strange feeling, as though the satin bed jacket had vanished, and there was only the thin silk of her night gown between them. She felt as though she was blushing all over.

"That does not sound like something you learned in England," she replied, trying to sound normal. "I rather suspect that you learned it last night."

"No," he stated emphatically, "I thought of it many years ago while you were still in the nursery. I thought at the time how lovely my mother looked against her pillows and I have never yet seen another woman who rivalled her."

"I wonder if your mother would be shocked at you being in my room while I have breakfast."

"I had almost forgotten for the moment that I was supposed to be your brother," he laughed. "But, now I think of it, we are merely acting our part sensibly and, if I *was* your brother, I should certainly be taking breakfast with you!"

"But as you are not my brother, I think you should go and have breakfast in the Saloon and when you return, I shall be dressed."

He seemed to become suddenly conscious of where he was and what she was wearing.

"Yes, certainly," he mumbled, rising to his feet and going slightly red. "I'll see you again later."

He walked out without looking back.

For a long time after he left Lexia lay staring at the door, full of thoughts and feelings that she did not understand.

"*You look very lovely in bed.*"

That was what he had said and it had taken her totally by surprise.

She could hardly remember what words she had uttered in reply – something stupid, she feared.

She only hoped he had not detected her confusion. She had tried to speak lightly, almost passing it off as a joke, but now that she was alone she realised that something very important had happened.

She smiled and snuggled down in bed, luxuriating in the feeling.

CHAPTER NINE

For the rest of the day they stayed together as the ship headed for Barcelona.

Just once they encountered Juanita as she was about to leave the ship and at the sight of her, the Marquis seized Lexia's hand, which was already tucked into his arm, making sure that she could not remove it.

She had no intention of removing it.

He smiled politely and Juanita cut him dead and then she flounced down the gangway.

"Let's go and enjoy ourselves in Barcelona," suggested the Marquis.

They took a carriage and spent a few happy hours exploring the beautiful old City, but when they were having lunch, he observed,

"You're not really thinking about where we are now, are you?"

Lexia sighed ruefully.

"You have seen through me. My mind has gone ahead to Greece as when I was very young my mother used to read to me about the ancient Gods and Goddesses. As I got older I started reading about them for myself, which rather annoyed my governess, who thought it was far more important for me to learn deportment and flower arranging."

"Who is your favourite?"

Lexia considered.

"I can never quite decide. Wise Athene, Apollo, the Sun God, Aphrodite, Goddess of Love – "

"Don't forget Ares, the God of War," he reminded her. "I always thought it fascinating that Eros, the God of Love, was born of Aphrodite, which you would expect. But his father was Ares and so he was the child of both love and conflict."

"Does that mean that the love he represents isn't perfect?"

"No, it means that it's human. Love and conflict go hand in hand in the world. My own parents had very hot tempers and they were always quarrelling so that people wondered how they could ever stay together.

"But the truth was that they loved each other deeply enough to see them through their fights. When my mother died my father was desolate. He only survived her by a year and then he had a heart attack and the doctor said if he could have written 'died of a broken heart' on the death certificate, he would have done so."

He looked into the distance for a moment.

"Perhaps that is one reason I could never take to any of the insipid females that were introduced to me. I could not imagine any of them telling me I was talking nonsense, which Mama used to say to Papa all the time."

"Perhaps you never talk nonsense?" observed Lexia wryly.

"Lexia, *please*!" he cried in disgust. "Not you as well."

She laughed aloud.

"No, I can be counted on not to flatter you, can't I?"

"Thank goodness," he said fervently.

They raised their wine glasses, watching the bright sun wink off the red liquid as they toasted each other.

"I cannot wait to get back to the ship and leave for Athens," enthused Lexia. "I have waited so long to see it and somehow I never thought I would manage it."

"I daresay a lot of people would feel the same."

"I am not sure as I think most people believe the old legends of Greece are fairy tales, but to me the Gods and Goddesses are very real."

The Marquis smiled at her.

"I too have always wanted to visit Greece," he admitted. "But there are many other countries I would like to see as well."

"I think I will be content with Greece," replied Lexia. "It's so lovely and I know it has helped and inspired people since the beginning of time and everyone needs help and inspiration."

"Ourselves, particularly," he agreed, "but afterwards, there is the whole world waiting to be explored and if we don't find what we are seeking almost at once, we will go on looking."

Lexia laughed.

"You forget, I have already found him."

His heart seemed to give an uncomfortable lurch.

"You have really found your true love?" he asked idly.

"Why, Mr. Storton, of course. I promise you, he's at my feet any time I want him, but the trouble is that I don't want him and I cannot make him believe it."

His heart resumed its normal rhythm.

"And there was I thinking that you had a preference for Alaric Carnoustie!"

"He has left the ship, somewhat earlier than he planned, I gather. I cannot think why."

"I can," muttered the Marquis grimly.

They eyed each other satirically.

"Perhaps you should give me back my blue feather," she laughed.

"I don't know what you mean."

"I think you do. Mr. Carnoustie had a word with me before he left the ship. A very interesting word. Where's my blue feather?"

"I am not sure you can be trusted with it. You seem willing to distribute your personal adornment to every man in sight and as your brother, I disapprove."

Lexia chuckled.

"Well, I haven't given one to Mr. Storton, although I know he'd like it."

"Is he making a nuisance of himself, because if so – "

"You may safely leave him to me," declared Lexia, her eyes teasing him.

"Hmm!"

She sighed luxuriously.

"Oh, this is lovely. Wouldn't it be nice to stay away from England so long that people forgot our very existence?"

"I fear there is no hope of that, but something may happen – " he seemed suddenly awkward, "something that makes it possible for us to drift on like this for a long time."

"I cannot think what that could be."

"Can't you?" he asked, a little sadly. "Can you really think of nothing?"

"It would take a miracle," she mused.

"But miracles do sometimes occur, don't they?"

"I think I've had all the miracles I dare ask for

recently. Once, everything looked so grim and now it's so wonderful. Asking for more might be tempting fate and the Gods might think we were being greedy."

The Marquis seemed to be occupied with looking into his glass.

"Surely we could ask for just a little more?" he suggested.

"More than this?" she teased. "Is there any more?"

"There might be," he said cautiously.

The Marquis was choosing his words with great care, trying to divine what was happening in her mind before going any further.

"When we came away we were only reluctant allies," she said, "and now we're good friends. That alone is far more than I dared to hope for and I won't risk asking for anything else."

"But you did just a moment ago, when you expressed a wish to go on like this forever," he reminded her.

"I was only thinking that it would be nice to be free to do as we pleased, without having to worry what anyone said, always to be able to slip away unnoticed."

"I don't think *you* could ever slip away unnoticed. Wherever you appeared you would fill the air with mystery and excitement."

She laughed.

"Thank you, kind sir, but it isn't true."

"I say it is."

"But we were talking seriously about Greece, where there is real mystery and excitement to be found."

"I still think you look very lovely. In fact I shall enjoy seeing you in Greece, which will be a perfect background for you."

"What a lovely compliment and one I will always

cherish. In future, when I look in the mirror I will ask if I look like a Greek Goddess or a rather ordinary English girl?"

He smiled and said no more. She no longer looked like an ordinary girl to him and soon the time was coming when he would tell her so.

*

They took the carriage back to the *Maybelle*, where the last of the new passengers had just boarded and instead of going to their rooms they lingered on deck, watching the activity of the sailors as they prepared to leave port.

The sun was setting as the *Maybelle* drew away from the shore and headed out to sea. The Marquis turned to look at Lexia trying not to alert her.

He enjoyed watching her while she was unaware of his attention and he loved to contemplate her beauty and the slightly wistful look on her face as she gazed out over the water.

He wondered if the look was a true indication of her feelings. Was she still sad about the man she had loved and lost and was it too soon for her to have put him into her past?

He hoped with all his heart that she had managed to do so, because there were words he was longing to say to her.

He was not quite sure when he had begun to realise that he was in love with her.

Perhaps it had started on the evening in the casino, when he had felt the stirrings of jealousy.

Or maybe it had been when he saw her looking so pretty in bed with her hair streaming over her shoulders.

She had been jealous of him too he had realised and she had not liked him spending so much time with Juanita. Had that been when he had begun to hope?

Or had the love been there from the first moment?

He was rather inclined to believe that it had.

He had fallen in love with her beauty and her irrepressible spirit. Now he could think only about her and he loved her for herself, caring nothing for her money.

In short he was the very man that she had set out to find, if only she could be brought to see it.

"What are you thinking?" he asked gently.

She turned and gave him a smile that melted his heart.

"Just – how beautiful everything is," she sighed. "And yet – I don't know how to say it – "

"Beautiful but strangely incomplete?"

"Yes," she said eagerly. "Something is missing, but I am not quite sure what it is."

"I feel that too. I sense it very often these days."

"We're very ungrateful to be discontented," she said. "We have so much."

"Yet perhaps we lack the one thing that really matters."

His heart was beating hard as he sensed his moment coming. Now, surely, he could tell her the feelings that came from deep in his soul and which were for her alone.

"Lexia," he began gently.

She looked up, giving him the smile that took his breath away.

It was hard for him to speak, knowing that the great event of his life had come. This was make or break and in a moment he would know his fate.

"Lexia," he said again.

"Yes, Frank?"

He drew a deep breath, gathering his courage.

And then her face changed.

She was looking at something beyond him and he saw her eyes widen and a look of incredulous joy came into them.

"Oh, my goodness!" she breathed.

He turned, trying to see whatever had made this transformation in her.

A man was standing by the rail.

He was very tall with thick fair hair and the look of a young God.

Lexia gave a little squeal of delight.

"*Wayne*!" she cried.

The next moment she had flown away from the Marquis's outstretched hand and was speeding along the deck to throw herself into the stranger's arms.

He saw her coming and a huge beaming smile spread over his ridiculously handsome face.

"*Lexy*!" he bellowed, enfolding her in his arms and holding her tight against his broad chest. "Dang me if it ain't my little girl!"

His embrace was so exuberant that he lifted her clear off her feet and swung her round and round in the air.

Her parasol fell to the ground unnoticed and the Marquis retrieved it as he walked quietly towards them and stood, waiting for one of them to notice him.

"Lexy," the stranger repeated over and over.

"Oh, Wayne, this is *so* wonderful."

The Marquis felt as though he had been swallowed up by an earthquake.

One moment he had been inching slowly but surely towards his goal and the next everything had been snatched away from him and he had been brutally reminded that she loved another man.

He wondered how he had allowed himself to forget the other man and now it all came back to him that Lexia had declared she would marry Wayne Freeman or die.

For a moment he knew a surge of anger. She had made a fool of him, using him as a way of travelling to meet her true love.

Then his common sense returned. It was he, not she, who had booked passage on this ship and she had known nothing about it until they were aboard.

To his relief the other two had finally finished their transports of delights, although Wayne was still murmuring, "Lexy, Lexy," which the Marquis thought a very ugly and unnecessary distortion of her beautiful name.

"Oh, no, Wayne, you must not call me that," admonished Lexia hastily.

"Why not? I recall your Daddy didn't like it, but you never minded. He ain't here, is he?"

"No, Pa's back in England. I am travelling incognito."

"Well, I'll be – ! Why?"

"It's a long story. You must have dinner with us and I'll tell you all about it. In the meantime, allow me to introduce my brother – "

"I don't remember you having a brother. In fact, your Daddy used to say that you were his only child and he was darned if he was going to see you married to some no-hoper with – "

"Wayne, will you hush and listen?"

"Sorry, ma'am."

He looked so sheepish that Lexia burst out laughing. He laughed with her and then they were in each other's arms again.

"Oh, it's so good to see you!" she cried.

"You really are sure your Daddy ain't here, 'cos if he saw us acting like this – never did know such a man with a shotgun."

The Marquis, eyeing them wryly, thought that a

shotgun might be a very good idea.

"Anyway, this is my brother, Mr. Edward Malcolm," said Lexia, indicating him. "I am his sister, Agnes – "

"You are?"

"No, of course I'm not really, but we're pretending."

"I think I'll go and dress for dinner," said the Marquis in a strained voice. He did not think he could stand much more of this. "Mr. Freeman – "

"Hey, you know my name!"

"My – er – sister, has mentioned you to me. I look forward to seeing you at dinner."

He gave them a brief bow and walked away.

Another few moments and he would have tossed Wayne Freeman overboard.

The last words he heard the man say was,

"Meeting you again is the most wonderful thing that ever happened to me."

He moved quickly out of earshot before he could hear any more.

"Can we go somewhere private?" Wayne asked at once. "I have so much to say to you."

"We can talk, but Wayne dear, if you're thinking – "

"Oh, lordy no! That was just your Daddy with windmills in his head. You've always been like a kid sister to me, but sometimes a guy needs a sister to help him out and this is just one of those times."

"Then let's go below and you can tell me all about it."

She took him straight below to her cabin.

"How did you come to be here?" she asked when they were safely inside. "I thought you were in America."

"I was, but I met this girl – she is the most wonderful, beautiful, incredible – "

Lexia listened patiently while he went on in this way for a few minutes, until at last he said with a sheepish smile,

"And she's also – hey, I guess I've said that already."

"Several times. Why don't you tell me her name?"

"Harriet Grant and she's English. Her father's a diplomat and he was in the States as third Secretary at the Embassy, but since then he's been sent to Greece as the *first* Secretary of the Embassy in Athens.

"He's an important man – at least, he thinks he is and he wasn't going to let her marry me, no sir! I told him I've got plenty of money and I could give her a really comfortable life, anything she wants. But he wants a title for her."

"It's a common affliction," murmured Lexia. "She has my sympathy. Does Harriet love you?"

"Oh, yes, she definitely does. When her father took her off to Greece I told her I'd come for her and that's what I'm doing."

"You're going to meet her in Athens?"

"That's right, if I can do it without attracting too much attention, but if I get recognised, he'll put guards around her."

"And you might just be recognised," mused Lexia. "You're so tall and – well, handsome, I suppose."

He grinned ruefully.

"Gee, thanks!"

They laughed together.

"What about Mr. Malcolm?" he asked. "If that's really his name."

"What makes you think it isn't?"

"Well I sure as heck know that you aren't called Agnes Malcolm. So what's *he* called?"

"That's a secret."

"Are you two eloping?"

"Certainly not. He's like a brother to me."

"I thought *I* was your brother," said Wayne, slightly hurt.

"You too."

"You sure do collect brothers, don't you?

"We want to find love," explained Lexia, "and isn't that what everyone wants? People keep trying to marry us off to each other."

"And you don't want that, huh?"

"Neither of us wants it," replied Lexia in a carefully colourless voice. "But as brother and sister, we can help each other."

"Does that mean you can't help me?"

"Of course it doesn't. But what can I do for you?"

"Hide me."

"All six foot four of you?" she could not help saying.

"I wouldn't ask if there was anything between you and that guy, but if he's supposed to be your brother then we could pretend to be – you know – "

"Just as far as Athens?" she supplied.

"Right. Then nobody will get suspicious of me until it's too late."

"What counts as 'too late'?"

"There's a ball in Athens and it's a big occasion with most of the diplomatic community there and they always issue tickets to the First Class passengers from these ships, if they happen to be in port."

"Hence your presence on the *Maybelle*?"

"That's right. Harriet will be at the ball and we're going to elope. It's all arranged. We've been managing to write to each other, but it's difficult over such a long distance.

"Her last letter reached me three weeks ago, telling me about the ball and hoping I could come for her. I wrote back, promising to be there, but I don't know if she received it or perhaps her father intercepted it and will keep her away.

"But I have to be there, just in case. So I will arrive by this ship and if I could go as one of your party, we might fool him. You will help me, won't you?"

"Of course I will and I know Edward will too. Let's meet at six o'clock in my cabin."

Wayne jumped up, gave her an enthusiastic hug and then he dashed out without another word.

He was like a playful puppy, Lexia thought, smiling tenderly. She would help him in any way that she could and be happy for him.

She dressed that evening in deep blue satin that made her blue eyes gleam like sapphires.

Wayne was the first to arrive and Annie admitted him with a sigh of admiration. The magnificence of his height and bearing had made an impression on her, as Lexia guessed it did on many women.

Tonight he was splendid in white tie and tails and he whistled when he saw Lexia, in a way that would have made her father wince and immediately produced a gift.

"It's just a little something to show how grateful I am," he said, holding up an exquisite diamond pendant. "Luckily the ship has a good jewellery shop."

"It's lovely and it will go so well with this dress. Put it on for me."

There was another knock on the door and Annie opened it to admit the Marquis, who crossed the threshold just in time to see Wayne fastening the pendant around her neck.

He halted for a moment to quell the revulsion of feeling in his breast. What shocked him most was the beaming smile of welcome that Lexia gave him and evidently she saw nothing wrong in being caught like this with a man in her room, bedecking her with jewels.

He chose to forget how he had sat on her bed while she lay in it, but that was entirely different. She trusted him as a gentleman and he had not betrayed that trust.

But Wayne Freeman was a man who had earned her father's express disapproval and no doubt Mr. Drayton had had his reasons.

With difficulty the Marquis stopped himself from scowling.

Seeing the pendant close up was like receiving a blow in the stomach. He had noticed it in the shop and recognised that he could never have bought it for her himself.

So Wayne Freeman was not after her money and that perhaps was the secret of his attraction for her.

At the thought of what he had been about to say to her that day he felt himself shrivel inside.

"Are we all ready to go to dinner?" he asked stiffly.

"Yes," said Lexia, "but first, we want to explain – "

"My dear girl," he interrupted her quickly, "why bother? Brothers aren't entitled to explanations. Shall we go?"

Upset by his tone, she assumed the same cool demeanour.

"Yes, I am very hungry."

As she spoke, she slipped her hand firmly through Wayne's arm and he patted it with a look of tender fondness.

The Marquis led the way out of the room.

Matters did not improve when the three of them were

seated at their table. Lexia was angry with the Marquis for having suddenly set her at a distance, but she would not allow him to see that this was making her unhappy.

Wayne looked from one to the other feeling apprehensive. He was not a subtle man and he lacked the social skills to deal with this situation.

"Lexy," he muttered, while the Marquis's attention was occupied by the waiter, "you don't think he's mad about me being here?"

"Of course not. I told you, he is just a brother to me."

The Marquis, trying to instruct the waiter and listen to them at the same time, heard only, "*he's just a brother to me.*"

So it was true.

This was the man she loved and had loved all the time.

He could not say that he admired her taste. To him Wayne Freeman appeared little more than an overgrown schoolboy, but he had the face of a Greek God and perhaps that was all Lexia asked.

He forced himself to try to appear civil.

"Will you be aboard the *Maybelle* for long, Mr. Freeman?" he enquired.

"Hey, call me Wayne. All my friends do."

"Indeed?"

"I'm headed for Athens. There's a big event happening there – a dinner and a ball afterwards."

"We can all go," came in Lexia. "Wayne says there will be some tickets set aside for the passengers."

"How delightful. Is the ball for any particular occasion?"

"It's concerning some treasure that's been discovered on one of the islands," Wayne told him. "There'll be a lot of collectors and historians."

"Are you an historian?" the Marquis asked politely.

"Me? No, I – er – I've got another reason for being there."

He shot a look at Lexia as he spoke and she interpreted his remark correctly as, 'you won't let me down, will you?' but the Marquis read something entirely different into it.

After the awkward meal was over they moved to the ballroom, where Wayne promptly begged Lexia to dance, as a way of removing himself from the Marquis's orbit.

"He's real heavy going, isn't he?" he commented as they circled the floor.

"He's just in a bad mood."

"Maybe he thinks there's something between us and he's jealous?"

The sudden leap of her heart warned Lexia that this was dangerous territory.

Surely Frank could not be jealous? That would be too wonderful to be true.

Suddenly she could not wait to find out.

"Let's go and sit down," she urged.

But when they returned to their table there was no sign of the Marquis and the waiter said that he had retired, leaving them a message to say goodnight.

CHAPTER TEN

They all awoke to find that the ship had already docked and before them lay the beautiful city of Athens, while in the distance they could just make out the Parthenon.

The Purser's Office had already received tickets for the dinner and ball that evening and the Marquis hastened to secure three, insisting that Mr. Freeman, as he persisted in calling him, was a guest.

Since this was precisely the kind of cover Lexia wanted, she said nothing, but she wished that the Marquis's manner was less forbidding.

In her mind she was calling him 'the Marquis' again. Somehow 'Frank' no longer seemed appropriate to this coolly dignified man.

One thing was certain – whatever she had hoped to say to him last night would have to wait.

About twenty of the ship's passengers were to attend the ball and carriages would call for them in the late afternoon.

Lexia spent the afternoon preparing her appearance.

Her dress was magnificent, made of pink satin heavily embroidered with beads and glittering thread. Tiny diamond ear rings nestled in her ears, a diamond tiara perched on her head and around her neck she wore Wayne's gift of the diamond pendant.

"You've done a wonderful job, Annie," she smiled. "You can go now, but be careful going round Athens alone."

"I shan't be alone, miss. That Hawkins will be with me."

"I thought you despised him."

"Well, I don't mind him making himself useful," replied Annie generously.

Lexia chuckled as Annie put on her cloak and departed.

The Marquis called for her first, looking every inch the English gentleman.

"You look delightful," he told her.

His eyes swept over the pendant, but he made no comment and before she could speak, he added,

"I was wondering whether to add a tie pin to my attire. I have one that I am very fond of, a gift from a dear friend."

For a moment they were able to smile together.

"Frank – "

But she was interrupted by a knock on the door. It was Wayne.

"Our carriage is just outside on the quay," he announced.

It was he who put Lexia's cloak around her shoulders, his eyes lighting on the pendant. The Marquis did not miss his smile of recognition and approval.

He tensed, but then forced himself to relax. He was determined to remain pleasant tonight. He had played the game of love and lost. He might not approve of his lady's choice, but he would at least behave like a gentleman.

On the journey Wayne seemed overcome by an attack of the fidgets. He coughed, looked over his shoulder, then at his watch and then at Lexia.

At last she leaned forward and took his hand.

"Wayne, please don't worry. It's going to be all right, I promise."

"Is there any trouble?" enquired the Marquis politely.

Wayne flung him a despairing look and Lexia hastened to calm him.

"There's no trouble," she insisted firmly. "Wayne, stop agitating yourself."

"I can't help it," he moaned miserably. "When I meet all those diplomatic characters I shall just sink into the ground. They make me feel small."

"What do you mean, 'diplomatic characters'?" the Marquis asked in sudden alarm. "I understood that this was an historical occasion celebrating an archaeological find."

"It is," Wayne explained, "but it's being staged by the British Embassy and the Ambassador will be there and several major diplomats. Does that matter?"

The Marquis ground his teeth.

"Of course it matters. I went to school at Eton, which is where most of the top staff of the Embassies attended."

Lexia's hands flew to her mouth.

"Oh, goodness, of course. There's bound to be someone there who will recognise you."

"The British ambassador to Greece is Lord Symons, an old friend of my father – and there will be others."

"What are we going to do?" asked Lexia, horrified.

"Mr. Freeman will have to go alone," said the Marquis firmly. "You and I must turn back."

"Oh, no, I simply must go," she replied at once.

"Lexia, it isn't possible," he came back firmly. "Once my true identity is known, how will we explain you – without causing a scandal?"

"But that's easy. We go in separately, you by yourself and me with Wayne. Nobody will connect us and there will be no scandal."

"There's no need for Lexy to turn back," persisted Wayne, taking a firm hold on her hand. "They won't know her?"

"Wayne's right," agreed Lexia strenuously. "He'll take care of me."

The Marquis felt a flash of bitterness at the way they united against him. They might as well announce their engagement here and now, he thought, but one thing was for certain. He had no intention of leaving them alone.

"Very well," he said through gritted teeth.

In all too short a time their carriage rolled up to the British Embassy and footmen emerged to open the carriage door. Lights poured from the inside.

"Are you ready?" enquired the Marquis as they approached the open doors. "From this moment on we do not know each other. We just happened to be travelling on the same ship."

As soon as they approached the Great Ballroom, Lexia understood how nearly they had fallen into a trap.

The Ambassador recognised the Marquis immediately, yelling,

"Francis! By all that's wonderful! Fancy meeting you here!"

The next moment their hands were clasped and they were laughing. The Marquis was greeting Lady Symons, who also recognised him.

"Who is that guy?" muttered Wayne.

"Lord Wimborton," Lexia told him.

"Is he a very high up sort of Lord?"

"He is a Marquis. That's only one step below a Duke."

"Gee! *Oh, lordy!*"

"What is it?"

"I've seen Harriet. Over there. The girl in green and that's her father with her. He's seen me. Play up to me, Lexy. Quick!"

She responded by giving him a dazzling smile, guaranteed to convince any onlooker that she was besotted with him and he returned her look in full measure.

When they turned away from each other, Lexia realised that the girl in green was staring at them, pale and horrified.

"Don't worry, I'll tell her," she whispered to Wayne.

Then they had reached the Ambassador and were giving their names, shaking hands.

First the Ambassador and his wife, then Sir Richard Grant, First Secretary of the Embassy, who regarded Wayne coldly and gave a sharp look at Lexia.

From the little satisfied nod of his head she gathered that he was convinced.

The first hurdle had been successfully cleared.

As they moved on to mingle with the throng, Lexia looked around for the Marquis, but he was nowhere to be seen.

In many ways this was the best thing that could have happened, she realised. It had forced her and Wayne to enter alone together, which was exactly what was needed.

But still, she wished she could see the Marquis somewhere. She felt lonely without him.

They were among the last of the guests to arrive and it was almost time for the dinner to begin.

She found herself seated next to Wayne and Harriet was close enough to turn burning, reproachful eyes on them. Now Lexia could see the Marquis, but he was carefully taking no notice of her.

Somehow she got through the meal, enduring the toasts and speeches which all seemed to go on for ever and when it was over, they were free to make their way into the ballroom.

"This is my chance," murmured Lexia.

"Are you sure you know what to say?" Wayne asked her.

"I have it by heart."

Harriet was moving away and now Lexia could see that she was going in the direction of the ladies cloakroom.

As soon as she had gone inside Lexia sped after her and sat down beside her at the long mirror. Harriet gave her a look of tearful outrage and would have moved away had not Lexia detained her with a hand on her arm.

"I come with a message," she said dramatically. "Wayne loves you. Only you and that's why he's here tonight."

Harriet stared.

"Then who are you?"

"I am his disguise. If your father thinks he's with me, he won't get too suspicious."

"My father is full of suspicion," moaned Harriet. "He wants to take me away early, before I can even speak to Wayne."

"Then you must leave at once," insisted Lexia firmly.

"But how can I?"

"When we go out, stay with me. Be very friendly. Laugh and talk. Don't even look in Wayne's direction and your father will see only that you are talking to another woman.

"When I move away, come with me. We will leave and depart in one of the carriages that brought us here.

Wayne has another carriage waiting a couple of miles along the road and you and he will change into that one, leaving me to go on to the ship."

"I will do everything you say," vowed Harriet nervously.

A few moments later they emerged together, arm in arm and engaged in vivacious talk. Looking around, Lexia could see that they were attracting no particular attention.

Sir Richard Grant glanced up once but, seeing that his daughter was not in Wayne Freeman's company, returned his attention to a diplomat from another Embassy.

While his back was turned Lexia grabbed Harriet's hand and pulled her through a side door.

"You'll have to lead me from here," she urged.

Harriet began to run with Lexia scurrying to keep up with her.

Then they were in sight of the front door. It was standing open and they hurried out.

Suddenly behind them Lexia heard a cry,

"I say! Wait!"

"Run!" she urged Harriet.

The two girls picked up their skirts, sped out of the door, down the long wide path to where a closed carriage was waiting all ready to go.

From behind came the cry of,

"Wait for me!"

The door of the carriage was opening and dimly they could see Wayne inside watching Harriet's approach, eyes filled with heartfelt love.

He leaned out to embrace her while she was still outside.

"We've no time for that," screamed Lexia. "Hurry,

there's somebody behind us."

She could hear footsteps catching up with them.

Wayne immediately pulled Harriet into the carriage and next Lexia.

But the brief delay had been fatal as before he could close the door behind Lexia, it was wrenched open again and another person hurtled in to land on the floor.

As the carriage started moving they all stared aghast at the newcomer.

"Mr. Storton!" exclaimed Lexia in disgust.

"I say, steady on, you might have waited for me?"

"Who the devil are you?" demanded Wayne violently.

"Sam Storton. I am a very good friend of this young lady."

"She doesn't seem to think so," responded Wayne belligerently. "Shall I throw him out, Lexy?"

"No, there's no time," she told him anxiously. "Hurry."

Sam Storton hauled himself up and sat down beside her. Inwardly she groaned, but she would deal with him later. For the moment Wayne and Harriet were her first concern.

For a couple of miles they were locked in each other's arms and then Wayne leaned out of the window and called,

"Here!"

The carriage halted. Both Wayne and Harriet thanked Lexia fervently and embraced her before climbing out. Wayne cast an uncertain look at Sam Storton.

"I'll be all right," she assured him.

They hurried away and Lexia saw them jump into a waiting carriage and she knew that Wayne had been ashore that afternoon to make all the necessary arrangements.

Then the carriage started up again and she was alone with Mr. Storton.

"Well, this is very nice," he said a blurred voice.

Lexia sighed, telling herself that it was only a short distance to the ship and she could put up with him for a little while.

He was not very sober and insisted on trying to squeeze her hand. Exasperated, she slapped him with her fan, only to provoke the response, "naughty, naughty!"

"That's nothing to what I'll do if you don't leave me alone," she threatened.

After that she fended him off as best she could and at last he seemed to take the hint, relapsing into the corner, giggling to himself.

When the carriage drew up on the quay she jumped out and raced on board, hoping to escape him, but he was right behind her.

As soon as they were on deck he grabbed her hand and pulled it through his arm.

"I will look after you, my beautiful one," he cooed.

"I can look after myself," Lexia told him sharply.

But he only tightened his hand and she was unwilling to make a scene in front of the passengers she could see taking a final stroll in the moonlight. Too late she wished she had been sensible enough to stay at the ball and return later.

'But I will be all right,' she thought as they reached her cabin and she opened the door. 'Annie will be here and – *oh, no*! *She isn't here.*'

Too late she recalled that she had given Annie the night off and she would have to manage alone.

She tried to push her way past Storton, who was still holding on to her arm.

"Goodnight," she said, "and thank you for bringing me

here."

"I'm not leaving you," he replied in a drunken voice.

"Oh, yes, you are."

Moving fast Lexia managed to slip away from him just long enough to get inside and slam the door in his face.

"Let me in, my darling," he yodelled.

"Go away!"

To her horror he began to thump the door, harder and harder. It bulged under the strain, but the lock held.

But for how long?

If only somebody would hear the noise and come to investigate, but there was nobody in this part of the ship tonight. They had all gone ashore.

Her only hope was that the Marquis would arrive soon.

She stared at the door as another thunderous hammering made it bulge again.

*

At last the Marquis forced himself to look around for Wayne and Lexia and that was when he realised that they were no longer present.

Enquiries elicited the information that neither of them had been seen for at least an hour.

So that was it – they had run away together.

Or perhaps they were back at the ship this minute, packing their bags, ready to depart before he could catch them.

In a moment he was out of the ballroom, running down the drive. He seized the first carriage he found and ordered it to race him to the ship in record time.

All the way there he was wondering just what he would find when he arrived.

He ran on board and headed down to their cabins as

fast as his feet would carry him.

With a few yards still to go, he heard Lexia scream and the sound galvanised him to run even faster.

The door of her room was open, hanging drunkenly on its hinges, as though it had been kicked in.

Inside was a sight that filled him with rage.

Lexia was lying on the bed, fighting a man whose face the Marquis could not see. Already he had her partially undressed.

"Leave her alone, damn you!" he roared.

Seizing the man by the back of his collar, the Marquis pulled him from the cabin and into the corridor.

He was struggling but a punch to his chin made him crash onto the floor. Instantly the Marquis hauled him up and for the first time he had a good look at his face.

"You!" he exclaimed as he saw it was Storton. "Then where – ?"

He dropped Storton, who fell into a crumpled heap and ran back to Lexia. She was sitting on the edge of the bed, holding her torn dress, which Storton had pulled from one shoulder, and weeping with shock and fright.

The sight enraged him.

He sat down beside her and pulled her quickly into his arms.

"It's all right, my darling," he murmured. "It's all right. I am here and I won't let anyone hurt you."

"Oh, Frank – Frank."

"Yes, yes, Frank's here and he'll look after you as much as you'll let him."

"Never leave me," she cried passionately.

"I never will – until you say that you want me to."

He folded her in his arms, rocking her back and forth.

"Whatever happened?" he asked tenderly. "Where is Freeman? I thought you left with him."

"I did, but Harriet Grant was with us. Her father is a diplomat at the Embassy and he wouldn't let them marry, although they're terribly in love."

"*They're* in – ?"

"Yes. Wayne begged me to help him, because we have always been such good friends, so of course I said I would. Harriet slipped out of the Embassy with me and Wayne was waiting for us.

"Everything went beautifully until that horrible man forced his way into the carriage with us. When Wayne and Harriet got into another carriage, I thought I could cope with him, but I think he must have been drunk.

"He followed me down here and tried to force his way into my cabin. I managed to lock the door against him, but he battered it down and thank goodness you came when you did."

She shuddered and nestled closer to him.

"But what are you telling me? You helped them elope? You don't mind that Wayne loves *her*?"

"Of course not. I am very happy for them."

"But you told me – "

"Wayne and I flirted a bit once, but there was never anything in it. Then Pa came down on us and said he would never let us marry. We didn't want to marry, but he wouldn't believe it."

"But didn't you tell him that you would marry Wayne or *die*?"

"Certainly *not*," she retorted indignantly. "I would never say anything so spineless."

"But when you saw him, you threw yourself into his

arms."

"Of course. I am very fond of him, but that's all. He's like a lovely big brother."

"I am supposed to be your brother. But oh, my darling, I don't feel at all brotherly towards you."

On those words he tightened his arms and kissed her fiercely, allowing her no chance to refuse.

But she did not want to refuse. This was not the lofty Marquis – it was her darling Frank, kissing her as though he had longed to kiss her forever and nothing was going to stop him now.

She knew exactly how he felt because she was not going to be prevented from kissing him too by any power on earth. It was only now that she knew how badly she had wanted him, longed for him, dreamed of him.

As the Marquis's lips met hers he became conscious of a strange feeling within him, which he had never felt before. His kisses deepened and he realised joyfully that she was kissing him back.

He was possessed by a delight that he had never known before.

For Lexia it was what she had always wanted, but thought she would never find.

The Marquis's arms tightened round her and his lips became very demanding.

It may have been only a short time or a long time. Neither of them could remember.

But when the Marquis raised his head, he said in a voice which did not sound like his own.

"*I love you*! I love you and I know I have loved you for a long time."

He did not wait for an answer, but kissed her again.

It seemed to him a long time later that, still with his

arms round her, he raised his lips from hers and said again,

"I love you! I know now this is what I have searched for all my life."

"I – love – you too," Lexia whispered so he could hardly hear her.

"You love me?" he exclaimed in astonished delight.

"I have loved you for ages," she managed to say, "but I thought you would never love me."

"I tried to tell you of my love yesterday, but then you saw Wayne Freeman and were so overjoyed that I was convinced that I had no hope."

"Was that what you were trying to say to me?" she asked in wonder.

"Of course it was, but I had to be careful about approaching you. I knew you trusted me and if you did not care for me, then I would have betrayed your trust and made it hard for you to travel with me."

"I was so jealous when you were with the Señora," she confessed.

"Do you think I could look at another woman once I had found you? Tell me that you love me and let me hear you say it."

"*I love you*," she said simply. "I love you with all my heart."

She hid her face against his shoulder and he tightened his arms.

"Are you absolutely sure," she asked, "that I am really the woman you want?"

"I adore you!" the Marquis replied firmly. "I know this is love. When your lips touched mine I felt as though I had come home to the place where I truly belonged and, my darling, we are going to be very happy together."

He kissed her again.

"I love you! I worship you!" Lexia murmured. "I did not know love could be so wonderful and so perfect."

"Tell me that you'll marry me quickly," he begged. "Here. Immediately."

Lexia looked up at him.

"Marry you – *here*?"

"If we go home there will be such a lot of people talking about us, saying they had always known we were suited to each other and that we really should be grateful to them."

Lexia gave a laugh.

"That does sound a bit like our friends and my father!"

"So we are going to avoid all that," said the Marquis. "If you agree we will be married here."

"That would be wonderful. Oh, but Frank – how can we marry here? We're both travelling with false passports. How can we prove our identities?"

"The Ambassador knows me and I think he will accept my word for who you are. We can be married in the Embassy and will spend our honeymoon in Greece, seeing the Gods and Goddesses, who perhaps played their part in bringing us together.

"Then I can teach you about love and we will be the happiest couple who ever existed. We have been seeking love without realising that it was so close to us."

He paused and smiled as he added,

"We will be joined even closer to each other once we are married."

"I think I must dreaming," sighed Lexia. "This cannot be true. Oh, Frank darling, I have loved you for so long, but would not admit it even to myself. Now I will do everything in my power to make you happy."

"You are making me happy already, just by loving

me," said the Marquis. "I love you from the top of your head down to your little feet. I worship you and I will spend the rest of my life trying to make you happy."

"I was so afraid that some other woman would snatch you away and you would forget about me."

"I will never forget about you. Instead we will become nearer and nearer to each other until we are one person. Nothing and no one will ever separate us."

"I just cannot believe it. Is it really true or am I just dreaming?" asked Lexia.

Then the Marquis was kissing her.

Kissing her so that it was impossible for her to speak or to think.

*

The following morning they left the ship and drove to the British Embassy where, as he had foretold, Lord Symons welcomed them and made no problems about their marriage.

They were married by the Chaplain in the Embassy Chapel.

"Do you know," Lexia whispered to him later that night, as they lay in each other's arms, "during the service I had the strangest feeling that unseen presences were watching us."

He held her close to his heart.

"I sensed them too," he said.

They smiled, each knowing who their guests had been.

Wise Athene. Apollo, the Sun God. Eros and Aphrodite, the Gods of Love.

They would be blessed and blessed again for Eternity and beyond.